**"Didn't mean to startle you again,"
the cowboy said in his slight southern drawl.**

He held a huge bouquet of roses. Dragging off his
Stetson, he added, "I'm Dalton Corbett."

"Georgia Michaels," she said, taken off guard.
He smiled. "Don't worry, I've only come in to
apologize and give you these as a peace offering."
He held out the flowers. "I am truly sorry for the
way I behaved yesterday." She smiled in spite of
herself. "Thank you," she said, taking the flowers
even though she didn't deserve them.

Dalton Corbett, along with being movie-star
handsome with thick dark hair and bright blue
eyes, was also gracious and quite charming.
Slipping his Stetson back on his head, he tipped
his hat to her.

"It was nice meeting you, Georgia Michaels."

BIG SKY DYNASTY

BY
BJ DANIELS

First published in Great Britain 2010
Harlequin Mills & Boon Limited,
Eton House, 18-24 Paradise Road, Richmond, Surrey TW9 1SR

© Barbara Heinlein 2009

ISBN: 978 0 263 88273 5

46-1110

Harlequin Mills & Boon policy is to use papers that are natural, renewable
and recyclable products and made from wood grown in sustainable forests.
The logging and manufacturing processes conform to the legal environmental
regulations of the country of origin.

Printed and bound in Spain
by Litografia Rosés S.A., Barcelona

ROM
Pbk

BJ Daniels wrote her first book after a career as an award-winning newspaper journalist and author of thirty-seven published short stories. That first book, *Odd Man Out*, received a 4½ star review from *Romantic Times BOOKreviews* magazine and went on to be nominated for Best Intrigue for that year. Since then she has won numerous awards, including a career achievement award for romantic suspense and numerous nominations and awards for best book.

Daniels lives in Montana with her husband, Parker, and two springer spaniels, Spot and Jem. When she isn't writing, she snowboards, camps, boats and plays tennis. Daniels is a member of Mystery Writers of America, Sisters in Crime, Thriller Writers, Kiss of Death and Romance Writers of America.

To contact her, write BJ Daniels, P.O. Box 1173, Malta, MT 59538, USA, or e-mail her at bjdaniels@mtintouch. net. Check out her web page at: www.bjdaniels.com.

This one is for knitters everywhere,
especially to the newest to the craft, seven-year-old
Miss Teagan Lynn.

Chapter One

"*Can you keep a secret?*"

Her whisper is husky in the dark.

He breathes her in, the sweaty air around her naked body fragrant with musk and the aroma of sex. Drunk on her, intoxicated by her body, her voice, her smile, he grins to himself in the dark.

A fingertip trails down his chest, the nails long and red as blood. "*Can you?*"

"*Sure,*" *he whispers back, eyes drooping as if he's been sedated.*

Her lips brush his neck, her long dark hair tickling his bare flesh, her touch dragging him out of his stupor to semiconscious desire. "*Could you keep a secret even if you knew it could get you killed?*"

Dalton Corbett shot up in bed fighting to catch his breath, the nightmare following him. Rationally, he knew his mind was playing tricks on him, but he could still hear the cry of the gulls, the lap of the water against the side of the gently rocking boat, the soft murmur of her whisper next to him.

Breathing hard, his skin soaked with sweat, he rubbed a hand over his face and dared to look at the other side of the bed.

Empty.

His heart thudded against his ribs. For one terrifying moment, he'd thought he'd find her lying next to him, her body limp, hair wet and lank as seaweed.

Just a nightmare. But so real he swore he could smell her musky perfume and he knew that if he touched her side of the bed, he'd find it still warm. He glanced down at his chest, half expecting to see where her nails had left rivulets of dried blood.

He looked to the window and saw not rolling ocean swells, but undulating vibrant green grasslands as far as the eye could see.

Still the nightmare surrounded him with an ominous dread. He'd thought he'd exorcized Nicci from his life, his thoughts, his dreams. He'd thought he was through catching glimpses of her in passersby on street corners or in cars speeding past.

That was until three months ago when he'd seen her in the back of a taxi in downtown Houston. A week ago it had been on the national television news. Yesterday it had been in Whitehorse, Montana, just miles from the ranch.

Swinging his legs over the side of the bed, Dalton headed for the bathroom to splash cold water on his face. Unlike his brothers, he'd been relieved when he'd gotten the call from his father, asking him to come to Montana to discuss some family business.

Trails West Ranch, hours from the nearest town with a commercial airport, couldn't have been farther away from his former life. He'd found peace here on the north central Montana working cattle ranch his father had recently bought. The closest town was the small western town of Whitehorse, which some people would argue was still far from civilization.

Like the outlaws who'd holed up in this area over a hundred years ago, he'd been happy to hide out here. He'd thought there wasn't a chance in hell that he'd see a soul who resembled Nicci Angeles in this untamed, remote part of the state where the Missouri River carved a deep gorge through the land on its way to the Gulf of Mexico.

He knew it was crazy even *thinking* he'd seen her in a taxi in Houston or on a national television news program. But crazier still to think he'd glimpsed her driving past in Whitehorse.

The woman he'd seen hadn't even looked like Nicci. Her hair had been blond and chin-length—not the wild dark mane he remembered from his nightmares.

On the television late-night news she'd been wearing a baseball cap so he hadn't even gotten a good look at her face. But there had been something about her that caught his eye. It couldn't have been Nicci being led away by two police officers, so he hadn't paid attention even where in Tennessee the crime had taken place.

What made him angry with himself was that after nine years, he'd let these random sightings of some stranger set off the nightmares again.

Standing in the bathroom over the sink, he splashed more cold water on his face and was reaching for the towel when his gaze went to the mirror. He froze, heart taking off at a gallop. For just a split second he'd seen Nicci behind him.

His pulse quickened at the memory of her smile—and the knife she held in her hand. He quickly shut off the water, dried his face and hands, and returned to the bedroom to open the window.

Cool summer air blew in on a gentle breeze. The sun had just crested the horizon, golden and warm, its rays fanning out over the prairie to dazzle the dewdrops on the tall green grass.

Taking deep breaths, he soaked in the tranquil scene. After a few minutes, he could no longer feel Nicci in the room. No hint of her scent hung on the air. Nor was he ever going to wake up to find her next to him, he reminded himself. Or worse, standing behind him again with a murderous look in her eyes.

Because Nicci was dead.

He should know. He was the one who'd killed her.

GEORGIA MICHAELS moved around the In Stitches yarn shop admiring each of her students' work. The majority were close to Georgia's age, in their late twenties. More than half were pregnant. Several were grandmothers or mothers of expectant daughters and granddaughters. That's why Georgia had been offering so many knitted baby clothing classes.

Today her class was knitting a baby afghan. It was an easy pattern using large needles. Some women simply took to knitting as if it were second nature. Others looked as if they were in a boxing match, fighting the needles every inch of the way.

Georgia stopped to help her friend Rory still her arms, before moving on to help McKenna pick up a dropped stitch. Both friends were great with ranching and horses, but knitting had them bamboozled. Both were pregnant, Rory almost due while McKenna had only just found out the good news a few weeks before.

"You'll get it," Georgia encouraged her beginning knitters. "It takes a little while to feel comfortable with the needles. Knitting is a great stress reliever."

"Sure it is," McKenna said with a laugh and the others joined in.

Only Agnes Palmer sat quietly in the corner knitting as if born to it. Agnes took every knitting class offered. Georgia suspected the petite, slightly built elderly woman knew more about knitting than Georgia did, but took the classes for the companionship.

Georgia loved the chatter—and the wonderful sound of nothing but the soft clack of knitting needles once class started. These women took their knitting seriously and she could appreciate that.

Knitting was a safe place for Georgia where she loved to return every chance she got. She'd been taught by the woman who'd adopted her, an elderly woman she'd called Nana. Georgia loved the feel of the needles in her hands as the yarn magically turned into some creation of her imagination.

The smooth repetition of movement lulled and comforted her, and just the sight of new yarn filled her with the excitement of all the wonderful possibilities.

Glancing at the clock, she announced, "Okay, ladies, that's it for today, but you're welcome to stay and knit if you'd like."

Usually after an hour, most of her class couldn't wait to quit, fingers cramped, eyes aching, patience spent. But they would all be back, some with several inches done, others with mistakes to be fixed.

Georgia heard Jim Benson, the local delivery man, come in the back door of the shop and call to her. This morning she'd left both the front and back doors open to get a breeze moving through the shop. It was going to be a warm one.

"See you tomorrow!" Georgia called to her departing class. As she started to turn toward the back of the shop, she saw a woman she hadn't seen before standing in the front window peering at the Apartment for Rent sign she'd put up just that morning.

"Looks like you'll be unpacking boxes all day," Jim said, drawing her attention as he came in through the back door carrying his clipboard. "You want me to stack them up in the storage room or bring them up here for you?"

She gave him a grateful smile as she signed for her shipment. "Up here if you don't mind. Over near my shelves?"

"No problem." He smiled. Jim was a nice-looking man only a few years older than Georgia herself. "Just heard on the radio. Some weather's coming in this afternoon. Talking storm warning. Thunder, lightning and maybe even some hail. Pea-sized or larger." He shook his head. "The farmers aren't going to like this one bit." He turned then and headed for his truck to unload.

When Georgia looked toward the front window again, the woman was gone. Too bad. Georgia had hoped to get the apartment rented. When she'd bought the building for her shop, she'd been excited to find there was a two-bedroom apartment upstairs for her and a one-bedroom rental apartment just across the hall.

Even though yarn sales and the knitting classes were going well, she really could use the additional income from the rental. She'd only recently finished painting, decorating and furnishing it.

Jim brought in all the boxes of knitting material, stacking them in easy reach for her to unpack near her shelves. "That work for you?" he asked.

"Thanks, Jim. I really appreciate it."

He nodded and seemed to hesitate. She could tell the past few times he came in that he wanted to ask her out, but he was having trouble getting up the nerve. She could have helped him out, but she was too busy trying to get her business going to date right now.

"Well, then, you have a nice day. Watch out for that storm later," he said, but then something caught his eye.

Georgia turned to follow his gaze. The woman she'd seen earlier was back standing in front of the Apartment for Rent sign. Slim, pretty with chin-length blond hair, she glanced up and smiled. Georgia smiled back and crossed her fingers that the woman was interested in the apartment.

As DALTON DROVE into Whitehorse, he swore. He hadn't wanted to go into town and wasn't the least bit happy about it. As he drove, he rehashed the conversation he'd had that morning at breakfast with his family.

"I need you to go in for feed," Russell Corbett had said the moment Dalton entered the main house dining room.

The oldest of the five Corbett brothers, Russell had moved up from Texas with the family to help their father run the ranch. The rest of the brothers had come when their father had asked and ended up staying for a while.

Not everyone had been happy about their father's move to Montana. Mostly because it had come as such a shock. None of them had expected their father to remarry. For years after losing the boys' mother, Grayson had been too busy raising his sons. By the time the boys had reached their twenties, they just figured he would never marry again.

Then Kate had shown up one day at the ranch in Texas with a box of photographs. Kate had grown up with their mother Rebecca on a ranch in Montana, the Trails West Ranch, and thought Grayson might want the photographs. Kate had lost touch with Rebecca after their lives took different paths.

Grayson had fallen for Kate like a boulder over a bluff. Within months they'd married and he'd sold the ranches in Texas to move to Montana to buy a belated wedding present for Kate—Trails West Ranch, the ranch where she'd grown up. Her father had lost the ranch when she was twenty-two, shortly before his death.

At first, Dalton and his brothers had thought the marriage and move too impulsive. But seeing how happy their father was had changed their minds.

"Give him a chance to eat his breakfast," his father had said, smiling down the table at Dalton this morning. Grayson loved having his sons in Montana and so far he'd been able to keep them here.

"Everyone else is tied up today," Russell said, pushing his plate away. "Did you have something else you had to do this morning?"

Dalton had been looking forward to a hard day's work on the ranch, even if it meant mucking out the horse stalls or stacking hay. After the nightmare, the last thing he wanted to do was go into Whitehorse. He'd be looking over his shoulder the entire time.

"I was just planning to work around here," he'd said as he'd dropped into an empty chair and helped himself to Juanita's huevos rancheros, one of her specialties. The smartest thing his father had done was talk their Texas cook into coming to Montana with them.

"Why doesn't Shane pick up the feed and I'll do his chores for him?" Dalton had suggested, expecting his older brother to jump at it.

"You're on," Shane had said with a grin. "I'd much rather pick up feed from town than drive to Billings with Maddie to attend a wedding extravaganza at the Metra and spend the day planning our nuptials."

"You'd better not let Maddie hear you talking like that," Kate joked.

His brothers Jud and Lantry had chuckled but were too busy putting away breakfast to comment.

"I guess I'll be going into town." Dalton had finished his breakfast with a lot less enthusiasm as everyone headed in different directions for the day.

The summer day was bright and blue, not a cloud in the sky, making it hard to believe a storm was headed their way. The air smelled of dust and grasses. With his side window down and his arm resting on the ledge, he drove the two-lane dirt road north. The sky seemed vast, as endless as the rolling prairie. It felt good to be on solid ground after years of spending days at a time afloat on the Gulf of Mexico.

Whitehorse was miles from anything else. Its original town had started farther south, nearer the Missouri River Breaks. But when the railroad came through, the town took its name and moved north, leaving behind little more than a few houses in what was now called Old Town Whitehorse.

Dalton dropped the truck off at the store to have the feed loaded and, too antsy to wait around, walked down the tracks the few blocks to the center of town. It was one of those Montana towns that had as many bars as it did churches.

There was a weekly newspaper, the *Milk River Examiner,* a grocery store, a clothing and a hardware store, an old-timey theater that showed one movie a week and a lumberyard.

Parked along the main street that faced the railroad tracks were always more pickups than cars. This was ranching country and the talk in the cafés and the bars always came back to the price of wheat and beef, the promise of rain, the threat of hail.

Dalton was considering stopping in the Great Northern for a cup of coffee when someone caught his eye. Just up the street a woman stood in front of a shop window. She appeared to be interested in something in the window.

He'd seen Nicci stand like that when she knew she was being watched. Her head was turned away slightly—just as it had been on the late-night television news. Even though she was no longer wearing the baseball cap, he could see that it was the same woman.

Dalton felt himself stagger as if a crushing weight had been dropped onto his chest. Fighting to catch his breath, he stopped under the shade of the hardware store's awning to get control. The woman wasn't Nicci. She just reminded him of Nicci enough to take him back to when he was eighteen and thought he knew everything.

Nicci had taught him how little he knew, a lesson that had almost gotten him killed and left him more than a little distrustful of women.

She stood in front of a small shop called In Stitches according to the sign. He'd never paid much attention to the store since it sold yarn.

Determined to get a better look at the woman and put this foolishness to rest, he stepped from under the awning into the morning sun.

As he drew closer, the woman slowly turned her head toward him. Her look said she'd known he'd been watching her the whole time.

She wore a large pair of dark sunglasses that hid part of her face and obscured her eyes. Still he could feel her green-eyed gaze, cold as the Arctic.

Before he could react, she turned and ducked into the yarn shop.

GEORGIA HAD JUST OPENED another box of yarn when she heard the click of heels on the floor as someone hurried into the shop.

"Be with you in just a moment," Georgia called from behind the stacked boxes of yarn. She started toward the counter with a skein of cerulean-blue mohair yarn in her hand. The wool was soft and beautiful. She was smiling, pleased at the quality of her order, when she looked up to see the blond woman rushing toward her.

"Please, help me," the woman whispered. "There's a man chasing me."

Through the open front door, Georgia heard the sound of someone running down the sidewalk in their direction. She took a step around a display table toward the front door, thinking she could reach the door and lock it before—

A tall, broad-shouldered man of about thirty, wearing a gray Stetson, jeans, boots and a Western shirt, rushed in. She'd seen the cowboy before somewhere, but couldn't place him.

"A blond woman just came in here. Where is she?" he demanded between ragged breaths. He would have been handsome had his face not been twisted in such anguish.

Before Georgia could answer, he spotted the open back door and rushed through the shop to the alley. She held her breath as she looked around the shop and didn't see the woman anywhere.

The cowboy quickly returned from the alley, looking even more upset as he entered the shop and seemed to sniff the air.

"I know she came in here, so you had to have seen her. Blond, big sunglasses."

"I'm sorry but I was busy putting away yarn." Georgia held up the skein in her hand, indicating the stack of boxes piled in the corner against the wall of shelves with cubbyholes that displayed each type and color of yarn.

He glanced at the stack of boxes, then at her. His face was flushed and he was breathing hard. "You had to have seen her. Just tell me which way she went." He looked as if he wanted to shake the truth out of her.

"I already told you…" Georgia noticed that the man's big hands were balled into fists. She backed toward the counter where the landline phone sat. "Please, I think you should leave now."

"You don't understand. I have to know where she went." His gaze went to the door leading up to the second floor. "Where does that go?"

"Upstairs, but I keep that door locked. I would have heard if someone had tried to go up there."

"You wouldn't lie for a woman you don't even know, would you?" He moved to the door to the second floor and tried it. Locked.

"If you don't leave, I'll have to call the sheriff," Georgia said, putting down the yarn to pick up the phone. She punched in 911, watching him as she did.

"That won't be necessary," he said, taking a step toward the front door. "I'm sorry I bothered you." He turned, gaze scanning the shop again, and left with obvious reluctance.

Georgia hung up the phone before the sheriff's office answered as the man passed the shop's front window. She waited a few moments, then went to the front door to peer out. From down the block, he looked back once, but kept going.

She watched until he reached the feed store at the end of the street, went inside and came right back out to climb into a large truck with the words Trails West Ranch printed on the side.

It wasn't until she saw him drive by and disappear around the corner that she said, "You can come out now."

Chapter Two

The blonde rose slowly from behind the stack of boxes where she had been crouched. There was high color in her cheeks and her light eyes shone with an unnatural brightness.

"Is he gone?" she asked, a tremor in her voice.

Georgia nodded. "I saw him drive away."

The woman tentatively stepped out from behind the boxes. She was stunning, the kind of female who made men's heads turn and women catty with jealousy. She wore strappy sandals with tangerine-orange capri pants and a matching short-sleeved jacket over a crisp white blouse.

Her skin was deeply tanned. Around her neck hung a silver necklace with a tiny sailboat on it and on her slim wrist, three slim silver bracelets that jingled softly.

Everything about the woman seemed exotic.

Georgia stared at her, thinking she should know her because surely the woman was a model or an actress. She definitely wasn't from Whitehorse, which was small enough that if Georgia didn't know everyone by name, she knew them by sight.

"I can't thank you enough," the woman said. "You saved my life."

Was she serious? Georgia thought of the cowboy who'd just left. He must work for the Corbetts out on the Trails West Ranch. He'd definitely been upset, but *murderous?* She wondered what possible connection this obviously sophisticated woman and that rough-edged cowboy might have.

The blonde glanced around the shop before settling her gaze on Georgia. She had the most luminous green eyes that Georgia had ever seen. "I didn't mean to involve you in my troubles. Can you forgive me?"

"Of course," Georgia said quickly, trying to place the accent. European? "I'm glad I could help."

She stepped to Georgia, laid one cool hand on her arm and smiled brightly. "Thank you again. Would you mind if I went out the back way?"

"Of course not. But do you have a place to stay? I saw you looking at the Apartment for Rent sign."

"I *was* interested in the apartment." She bit down on her lower lip, those green eyes filling with tears. "I do need a place to stay and a motel is out of the question since that would be the first place he'd look for me."

Georgia could only assume she meant the cowboy. "I doubt he would look for you here again."

"I suppose not."

"It's none of my business but—"

"No, you have a right to know why that man was after me. Especially if I rent the apartment."

"Would you like to see it?" Georgia asked, changing the subject temporarily.

She brightened. "Oh yes, please."

NICCI WAS ALIVE! Dalton pulled the truck over at the edge of town, got out and threw up his breakfast in the weeds. He was shaking, his mind refusing to admit what his senses knew as truth. Nicci had somehow survived. Not just survived but was now in Whitehorse. And he knew what that meant.

If she was here after nine years of letting him believe she was dead, then he was in serious trouble. As if just crossing paths with Nicci wasn't trouble enough. His heart hammered at the thought. Knowing Nicci the way he did, he could only assume she'd come to finish what she'd started.

But why, if she'd been alive this whole time, had she waited nine years to come after him?

Shaking his head, he tried to make sense of this and couldn't. He knew he'd acted like a crazy man back there at the yarn shop. He'd scared that poor young woman so badly she'd been ready to call the sheriff on him—might even have called after he left.

He cursed under his breath. He'd done insane things from the first moment he'd met Nicci nine years ago and it had only gotten worse. Why did he think now would be any different?

He had to get control of himself. But how could he?

Nicci was alive and in Whitehorse and playing some game he knew would only get deadly given their history.

Lightning splintered the sky in an explosion of light that made him jump. The clap of thunder immediately following it reverberated through him, making the hair stand up on the back of his neck. He glanced at the greenish blackness of the clouds moving across the prairie toward him. Hail.

Quickly, he put the truck in gear and looked for the largest tree he could find. The feed was covered with tarps in the back, but the truck itself… Slushy raindrops sounding as hard as hail pelted the hood and roof, drowning out all other sound.

Dalton pulled the truck under a large overhanging limb and cut the engine just as pebble-sized hail began to bounce off the pavement next to him. The hail tore through the thick green leaves of the tree he'd parked under, pinging off the truck and covering the ground in icy white.

He turned his thoughts from Nicci, to the apparent owner of the yarn shop. The young woman was the classic girl next door with her short curly chestnut brown hair, big brown eyes and glowing skin. The kind of woman who would protect another.

He recalled the determination he'd seen in her gaze and cringed remembering how he'd called her a liar. But she *had* helped the blonde disappear. He wasn't sure how, just that she had. Understanding why didn't help given who they were dealing with.

Tomorrow he'd go back to the shop and apologize. Maybe he'd take her some flowers. Anything to get her to tell him where Nicci had gone.

With a start, Dalton came out of his thoughts to silence. As quickly as the hailstorm had begun, it was over, having moved on. He sat for a moment, listening to water drip from what was left of the tree's leaves onto the truck roof before he pulled out and headed for the ranch, knowing what he had to do. It was something he'd put off far too long.

Dalton hated asking. Grayson Corbett had raised five overly independent sons. All of them would rather chew nails than admit they needed help.

As hard as it was going to be, he dialed his brother's cell phone number and said without preamble when Lantry answered, "I need a lawyer. I'm in trouble. Serious trouble and I need your help."

AGNES PALMER hurried home after her knitting class, praying she could beat the storm. The weather service had updated the forecast and was now calling for hail.

Agnes's pride and joy was her tomato garden. She was known all around the county for growing the biggest, beefiest and most beautiful tomatoes anyone had ever seen and had been for years.

This year she'd outdone herself. Her tomatoes would win blue ribbons at the fair and have people talking for years, although that wasn't why she did it. She raised tomatoes because her husband, Norbert, God rest his soul, had loved tomatoes. It was her way of never forgetting the man she had married and loved for more than fifty years.

As she drove up in her yard, she saw the thunderhead at the edge of her field. Ignoring the weatherman's advice to stay inside and away from windows, she hurried to the back porch for her plastic tubs and hightailed it out to her garden.

She could hear the thunder rumbling. Flashes of lightning lit the darkening sky. The air smelled of rain, which would be bad enough, but hail would destroy her tomato crop and Agnes wasn't going to let that happen even if it killed her.

Clouds obscured the light, pitching the day into a premature darkness as she began to pick. She'd filled half a tub when a bolt of lightning lit the darkness in a blinding flash of light. Agnes glanced up at the angry sky and considered the danger.

But she still had too many tomatoes to pick. She wasn't leaving them to this storm. More determined than ever, she began to pick more rapidly, filling one tub after another and dragging them over to the oak tree her grandmother had planted so many years ago.

Her roots ran deep in this part of Montana and she took a certain pride in that just as she did in her tomatoes.

As she scurried back to the garden to save the rest of her precious tomatoes, the first drops of rain slashed down from the dark heavens. Large, heavy and icy, the raindrops hurt as they struck her thin back and shoulders.

She bent her head against them and thought of something pleasurable—her knitting classes. While she enjoyed knitting, it was Georgia Michaels who made the classes so enjoyable. Never having had any children of her own, Agnes thought of the loving, caring woman the way she might have a daughter or granddaughter.

Not that she didn't find something to like in everyone. She'd gotten that from her mother, who always said, "People are like gardens. While they need sunshine, water and a healthy dose of prayer, grace grows good gardens and people. Mind you remember that."

Agnes *had* remembered.

The rain soaked her to the skin, beating her slim back and running in rivulets off the brim of her garden bonnet.

She glanced at her watch. Only a few more tomatoes to go. A bolt of lightning lit the garden in a blaze of white light. The thunderous boom was deafening and directly overhead.

Agnes reached for one perfect, large tomato, perhaps the one that would take the blue ribbon this year. She never saw the lightning bolt that hit her.

GEORGIA PICKED UP her keys for the apartment from where she'd thrown them on the counter earlier before her class and opened the door to the second floor.

Leading the way, she climbed the stairs to the landing and unlocked the one-bedroom apartment door across the hall from her own. Stepping back, she let her prospective renter enter.

"Oh, it's wonderful," the blonde exclaimed. "Did you decorate it yourself? Of course you did. I saw how you decorated the shop downstairs. You have a real talent for it."

The woman moved through the small apartment admiring the things Georgia had done, making her flush with embarrassment and pleasure. She'd hoped to rent the apartment to someone who appreciated what she'd done to make it more comfortable and homey.

Georgia watched the woman step to the front window that looked out over the main street. Directly across the street was a small city park and past that the old train depot next to the tracks. The depot wasn't open, but you could still catch a passenger train from here that would take you to Seattle or Chicago and all points in between.

The woman stared out at the street for a long moment as if looking for the cowboy, but when she turned back to Georgia, her face was glowing. "It's perfect."

"I'm so glad you like it."

"I *love* it," she said excitedly. "You're sure you won't mind renting it to me? But you don't even know me." She took a step toward Georgia and, smiling, extended her hand. "Forgive me, I should have introduced myself before. I'm Nicci. Nicci Corbett."

"Georgia Michaels," she said, taking the woman's hand, her eyes widening as she recognized the name. *"Corbett?"*

AGNES PALMER came to lying in the soft dirt, soaked to the skin and staring up at the rain. She blinked and sat up, relieved to see that when she'd fallen, it had been between her tomato rows and she hadn't hurt either her plants or her tomatoes.

"How odd," she said as she saw the overturned tub of tomatoes and saw where her body had left an imprint in the freshly turned earth. What had happened?

She glanced at her watch, shocked to see that she couldn't account for the last twenty-two minutes.

"Strange indeed," she said as she bent to pick the largest

of the tomatoes and felt a little dizzy. Holding the tomato she stared at it, seeing it more clearly than she felt she'd ever seen anything in her life.

Hail began to pelt the cabbage patch, tearing through the leaves before bouncing along the ground toward her.

Agnes quickly righted her tub of tomatoes and lifting it into her arms, skedaddled over to the old oak. She wormed her way back in against the trunk, pulling her tubs of tomatoes with her and sat down, suddenly tired but content.

Smiling to herself, she reached into one of the tubs, took out a fat, juicy tomato and took a bite as she watched hail as big as gumballs ravage her garden.

It wasn't until later, when the storm passed and she went inside with her tubs of tomatoes that she caught sight of herself in the hall mirror.

Her salt-and-pepper short brown hair was completely white—and curly. She'd stood staring, stunned, then she'd smiled at herself in the mirror. She'd always wanted curly hair.

GEORGIA COULDN'T HIDE her surprise as she shook Nicci's hand. Everyone in town had heard about the five Corbett brothers. In fact, two of Georgia's friends had fallen for Corbetts.

"That man who was chasing me was Dalton Corbett," Nicci said. "He's my *husband*. Soon to be ex-husband if I have anything to do with it."

Instantly Georgia regretted offering the apartment. The last thing she wanted to do was get involved in a squabble between a husband and wife in the middle of a less than amicable divorce. From the look on Dalton Corbett's face earlier…

Nicci must have seen her doubts. "I love the apartment and appreciate the offer, but I can't chance that Dalton will come back here under the circumstances and upset you."

Georgia nodded, relieved, but also feeling a little guilty. "But I thought you said you couldn't go to a motel?"

"Please, don't worry about me," Nicci said. "You've already done so much. I never expected to see a friendly face in Whitehorse, not with my husband's family living here. I wasn't joking when I said you'd saved my life. I wasn't looking forward to spending possibly months here waiting for the divorce to go through without even a friend." She glanced away from Georgia to look wistfully at the apartment.

"I think you should stay here," Georgia said impulsively.

"Are you *sure?* I promise I won't let him know where I'm staying," Nicci said hastily. "There won't be any trouble."

"I'm not worried." Crazy, yes. Worried, well, maybe that, too. But Georgia felt as if she was doing the right thing. The woman needed help. How could she turn her out onto the street?

"Dalton is harmless. Unless you're married to him." She'd looked sad for a moment, but quickly altered her expression to one of delight as she looked around the apartment again. "You won't be sorry you befriended me."

Georgia laughed. "Please, I haven't done anything."

"Just saved my life, that's all. You think that is something I'm likely to forget?" Nicci reached into her big leather shoulder bag. "The sign out front said four hundred dollars a month, first and last month's rent, and two hundred for the security deposit."

"But you don't know how long you will be staying," Georgia said. "I suppose you could pay by the week…"

"I won't hear of it. You've been too kind already." Nicci counted out ten one hundred dollar bills into Georgia's hand and smiled jubilantly at her. "What a lucky day it was for me when I ducked into your shop."

LANTRY CORBETT was waiting for his brother in one of the guest cabins just down the road from the main ranch house. Like his brothers, he'd come home when summoned by their father, Grayson, fearing bad news.

Their sixty-year-old father, it turned out, was just fine. Happily married to Kate and loving the new ranch in Montana. The problem was that after years of being unable to go through his first wife's things, he'd finally gotten the courage, thanks to Kate.

Grayson had found some letters that his sons' mother, Rebecca, had written before her death. One had been to him, telling him of her dying wish to have each of her sons marry before the age of thirty to a Montana cowgirl. The other letters were addressed to her five sons. They were to be read on the day of their weddings.

Stunned by this revelation, the brothers had all been caught up in the emotion of this find from the mother they had never really known and had done something crazy. They'd drawn straws to see who would marry first rather than go by age.

Jud had drawn the shortest straw, but he'd managed to weasel out of it by finding the perfect cowgirl, Maddie Cavanaugh, for his brother Shane. Shane, who'd drawn a straw just to shut up his brothers, had drawn the longest one. But fate had stepped in and the next thing he knew he was in love with Maddie and was now engaged and planning their wedding.

In a rare turn of events though, Jud had fallen in love

just last month with a true Montana cowgirl, Faith Bailey. They were busy working on starting a stunt riding school on part of Faith's ranch. Both weddings were pending.

Lantry, who'd drawn the second shortest straw, was next in line to find a Montana cowgirl to marry, but everyone in the family figured he'd try some legal maneuver to get out of it.

"Whoa, you look like you've seen a ghost," Lantry said, opening the door to Dalton.

Dalton gave a humorless laugh as he stepped into the guest cabin and turned to face his brother. "I wish it *had* been a ghost."

"Well, sit down and tell me why the hell you need a lawyer," Lantry said. "You've never asked for my help before. Wait a minute. If this is about getting out of the marriage pact we all made…"

"I'm *already* married. I got married nine years ago and kept it a secret."

"You're joking."

"I wish I were."

"Where is your *wife?*"

"It's a long story."

His brother studied him for a moment, then said, "I think you'd better sit down before you pass out." Lantry stepped to the bar, poured them both a drink and shoved a glass of brandy into Dalton's hand.

Dalton took a drink, fortifying himself, and sat down. He dreaded this. It would be bad enough admitting the truth to a stranger, but to his brother Lantry?

"I can think of only one reason you'd get married and keep it a secret," Lantry said as he took the seat opposite his brother. "Tell me I'm wrong."

Dalton took another drink of the brandy. It burned all

the way down but it seemed to steady him a little. "She wasn't pregnant. She *drugged* me."

Lantry laughed, thinking he was joking. He sobered and swore. "You're *serious*."

"Yeah."

"What the hell? The marriage would be invalid if either party was under the influence of alcohol or drugs."

"And how do propose I prove that after nine years?"

"Not even a justice of the peace would have married you if he thought—"

"You don't know this woman or what she's capable of. I have no idea how she pulled it off but she did. I saw the marriage license."

Lantry shook his head. "So how exactly did you end up drugged and married?"

"I don't even know where to start."

"How about the beginning. Where'd you meet this woman?" Lantry asked. He'd put his law practice in Houston on hold for a while. It was clear to all five sons that their father wanted them in Montana to be closer to him and Kate.

It was still unclear what Lantry planned to do since his Houston law practice specializing in divorce was very lucrative. He'd go broke in Whitehorse, Montana, since the population—let alone the divorce rate—was low.

Not that any of them needed the money. Grayson had divided a vast portion of his fortune between them years ago. That was one reason nine years ago, Dalton had been in a bar in Galveston just down from where he kept his sailboat.

"I met Nicci in a bar in Galveston," Dalton began. "The moment I saw her I was like one of those cobras that comes out of the wicker basket to the sound of the flute. Later, I realized that she was the one who'd come after me."

Lantry shrugged. "The woman did a number on you."

Clearly he'd heard more than his share of stories like this one as a divorce attorney in Houston. He just hadn't heard one quite like this, Dalton would bet on that.

"To say Nicci came on strong is like saying getting hit by a freight train hurts."

"She targeted you, clearly knowing who you were."

Dalton cut his eyes to his brother. "Damn, I had no idea you were so cynical about women."

"Not *women. Marriage.* Come on, this one is a no-brainer. She pretended she'd never heard of Grayson Corbett, right? And the next thing you know you're married."

Dalton was shaking his head, although Lantry was right. Nicci *had* said she'd never heard of the Texas Corbetts and he'd believed her.

"She *did* come after me, but not for the Corbett money," he said. "Nicci's wealthy, the only heir to multibillionaire Nicholas Barron Angeles. Hell, she's richer than Dad."

"She told you this, right? And you bought it hook, line and sinker. Damn, Dalton, what were you thinking? Let me guess, you didn't sign a prenup."

"I told you, she *drugged* me. Anyway I was *eighteen.* I didn't have much and she was rich. So what would have been the point?"

"The point is that even if she wasn't lying through her teeth about how rich she was at the time, now it is nine years later. *Now* you have money and maybe she's blown all of hers, if she ever had it. The point is you're screwed."

Dalton realized Lantry might be right. Nicci could have blown through her fortune by now and was looking to pick up a little cash. That would explain why it had taken her nine years to show up in his life again. But when he thought of that dark, humid night on the water, he doubted Nicci's thirst for blood was monetary.

"So where has she been the last nine years?" Lantry asked.

Dalton shook his head. "I haven't seen her since our honeymoon at sea. We parted ways a few days in."

His brother looked surprised. "And you never heard from her, tried to contact her, thought about divorcing her?"

"I thought she was dead."

Lantry looked momentarily taken aback. "What made you think she was dead? No, don't answer that." He suddenly looked as sick as Dalton felt.

Dalton rose from his chair and stepped to the window to look out. The black clouds of the thunderstorm hung on the horizon. It must still be storming not far from the ranch.

"Do you believe in evil?" When Lantry didn't answer, Dalton turned to look at him. "Nicci's evil incarnate and now she's come to Whitehorse."

Lantry shook his head. "If she's in town, she isn't after your *soul*."

"I wouldn't be so sure about that."

Chapter Three

An hour after Georgia had closed the shop for the day she glanced up at the sound of a key in the alley door. For an instant, she was startled.

The door swung open, a gust of cool evening air rushing in before the door closed again. For a moment, she'd completely forgotten that she'd rented the apartment.

"Georgia?" Nicci called as she stepped into the shop.

"Over here." The only light was a small one near the shelves where Georgia was busy finishing unloading the boxes that had arrived that morning.

The day had gotten away from her. She'd called in Miss Thorp, her former spinster teacher, to watch the shop while she helped Nicci bring up her bags from her rental car and then had gotten caught up in visiting and helping Nicci get settled in.

Miss Thorp had been Georgia's typing teacher in high school. "You'll never be a typist," the spinster had told her repeatedly during the course. Georgia still didn't know Miss Thorp's first name since the woman refused to be paid for watching the shop.

"Sitting here isn't all that different from sitting at home," Miss Thorp had said. "I like the change of scenery."

As long as Georgia didn't get Miss Thorp started on the evils of computers, she proved to be the perfect part-time, occasional helper for the shop. Especially since she didn't mind being called in at the last minute and worked for free.

Since business was often slow between classes, Miss Thorp would sit and read, which was just fine with Georgia. The one time she'd had her help her with a shipment of yarn, the typing teacher had complained about the way Georgia was doing it.

Georgia had enjoyed visiting with her new renter. Normally, she was shy, especially around strangers, but Nicci set her at ease at once by getting her talking about her two favorite subjects, Whitehorse and knitting.

Their conversation had been interspersed with laughter and comfortable silences as Nicci set about moving in. For a woman not planning to stay long she had a lot of summer clothing.

"Thank you for keeping me company," Nicci had said at one point. "I feel as if I've known you forever. Is that odd?"

"No," Georgia said. "I feel the same way." And it was as if they'd only been apart and were now just getting reacquainted.

Georgia was thankful when Nicci didn't ask about the Corbetts. Anyway, she figured Nicci probably knew more about them than she did.

"Still hard at work just as I suspected," Nicci said now, smiling as she joined her. She carried what appeared to be two takeout containers.

Georgia caught the delicious smell of fried chicken. Her stomach rumbled and she realized she hadn't had anything to eat since breakfast.

"I brought you some dinner," Nicci said. "I doubt you

got a chance to eat today and it's all my fault for talking your ear off and not letting you get your work done."

Before Georgia could be polite and deny it, Nicci rushed on. "I hope you like fried chicken. I was walking by the Great Northern restaurant and I saw they had a chicken special. Chicken, JoJos and coleslaw with sour cream for the potatoes. I couldn't pass it up."

Georgia laughed. "My favorite. But there is no way you eat like that all the time and stay as slim as you are."

"You'd be surprised. I can't stand depriving myself of anything. It's one of my tragic flaws," she said and laughed. "Come on, you can't let me eat alone."

Georgia hesitated. She really had wanted to get the yarn all put away before the shop opened in the morning.

"Take a break and eat with me, please," Nicci pleaded. "I hate eating alone and I refuse to let you starve given how wonderful you've been to me."

Georgia couldn't have said no under the circumstances even if she hadn't been hungry. She could eat and finish up afterward.

"You had me at fried chicken," she said. "Thank you."

"I'll take it up. Meet me in my apartment?" Nicci said over her shoulder. "I also got us some wine."

They ate at the breakfast nook, eating the chicken and potatoes with their fingers, sipping the wine and talking.

It wasn't until later, feeling a little tipsy, Georgia realized she wasn't going to get her work done tonight.

Much later, she crossed the hall to her own apartment, smiling to herself. She'd needed this tonight. A workaholic, she was often too serious. Her friend Rory used to make her take breaks from work to do something fun, but since Rory's pregnancy and marriage—and Georgia's working on expanding the yarn line at the shop—she had seen little of her best friend except at knitting class and as Rory's backup at Lamaze class.

Georgia hadn't realized how much she'd missed girl talk with Rory. Spending time with Nicci today made her all the more aware of how much she'd missed her best friend.

She vowed to make plans to get together with Rory outside of knitting and Lamaze classes.

THE NEXT MORNING, waking up a little hungover from the wine she wasn't used to drinking, Georgia realized with chagrin how much she'd told her new renter about herself.

After a few glasses of wine, Georgia had shared practically her entire life history. She blamed the alcohol and the fact that Nicci had a way of drawing her out, making her so comfortable, that she wasn't hesitant to talk about herself.

"The woman would make a great interrogator," Rory said when Georgia called her to tell her about her new renter and her embarrassment over last night.

"She's just so easy to talk to."

"So what did you learn about *her?*"

Georgia thought back and was even more embarrassed to realize Nicci had said little about herself. "I was so busy talking about myself apparently…"

Rory laughed. "That is so not like you."

"I know. It's weird. But you'll see what I mean once you meet her. She's really fun. You can't help opening up to her. It's like I have always known her."

"How long is she staying in town?" Was that jealousy she heard in her best friend's tone?

"I don't know. She's rented the apartment for a month. I guess it will just depend on how long her business here takes."

Even though Rory was her best friend and they told each

other everything, Georgia didn't feel it was her place to discuss her renter's personal business.

"This amazing woman has *business* in Whitehorse?" Definitely jealousy. "I can't believe you don't know where's she from, what she does for a living, what she's doing in town," Rory said.

"I got the feeling she's been living abroad. I don't know that she *does* anything. She seems to have a lot of money."

"Didn't you look at the check she gave you for the apartment? That would at least give you an idea where she banks anyway."

"She paid in cash."

"A thousand dollars? Don't you find that a little unusual?"

"No, obviously she'd seen the sign and knew how much she needed to rent the apartment," Georgia said, getting annoyed. "She probably thought I wouldn't take an out-of-town check."

"Sounds like the woman at least didn't just stumble in off the street," Rory said. "She had to be planning to rent the apartment if she had the money ready. I suppose that's good news. Still, you have to wonder what a woman like that is doing in Whitehorse."

Nicci *had* kind of stumbled into the shop, Georgia thought. But only because she'd been outside looking at the For Rent sign. And a woman like Nicci Corbett probably wouldn't think a thing about carrying around a thousand dollars in cash.

Rory was just jealous.

Once Rory met Nicci, she would like her and stop this.

"I'd better get busy," Georgia said, a little irritated with Rory. She'd called her friend to see about getting together, but now let it go. "See you at knitting class later?"

"Are you kidding? I can't wait. I have to meet your new renter."

MORNINGS WERE USUALLY slow at the shop and Georgia was thankful for it today. The summer day got remarkably hot fast. Just as she had yesterday, Georgia had opened both the front and back doors and had fans going. Few people in Montana had air conditioning since it was needed for such a short period of time each year.

But this morning with all the work she had to do, she would have loved the convenience. Her biggest problem though was that she couldn't get her conversation with Rory out of her mind.

What bothered her most was that Rory was right. Georgia didn't know anything about the woman she'd rented the apartment to. She had an application form that she'd planned to use for any interested renter, but she'd forgotten to get Nicci to fill it out. Now she felt funny about asking her to do it since Nicci had already moved in and wouldn't be staying long anyway.

Georgia was bent over one of the bins of yarn when she heard someone behind her. Straightening as she turned, she was shocked to see who.

"Didn't mean to startle you again," the cowboy said in his slight Southern drawl. He held a huge bouquet of roses. Dragging off his Stetson, he added, "I'm Dalton Corbett."

"Georgia Michaels," she said, taken off guard.

He smiled. "Don't worry, I've only come in to apologize and give you these as a peace offering." He held out the flowers. "I truly am sorry for the way I behaved yesterday."

She smiled in spite of herself as she rose to her feet. He looked genuinely apologetic and she felt horribly guilty. He'd accused her of lying yesterday—and had been right.

"Thank you," she said, taking the flowers even though she didn't deserve them. "This really wasn't necessary."

"It was and if there is anything else I can do, I'd be most

happy to do it," he said. "My behavior was inexcusable yesterday. I was upset. I thought I saw someone…someone I knew but didn't expect to see here in town."

She felt a wave of sympathy for him. No man got as upset as he had yesterday unless he loved his wife. That made Georgia feel even worse since she knew Nicci had come to Whitehorse only to divorce the poor man.

"Please, don't give it another thought, and the flowers were very thoughtful." Georgia could see what Nicci had seen in the man. Dalton Corbett, along with being movie-star handsome with thick dark hair and bright blue eyes, was also gracious and quite charming.

Yesterday Georgia had found his height and muscled arms and broad shoulders intimidating. Is that why Nicci had been afraid of him?

He certainly didn't seem dangerous now. If anything Georgia found him gentle. But then Nicci had said he wasn't dangerous to anyone except her.

Georgia couldn't help but notice also that his hands were calloused and his skin tanned dark from the sun. This was a hardworking man, not an idle rich one as she'd assumed when she heard about the Corbetts and their wealth and land.

"Apology accepted then?"

"Apology accepted," Georgia said.

He smiled so broadly that she felt as if the entire room had lit up. "Thank you." His gaze locked with hers for a moment, then acting almost embarrassed, he'd glanced around the shop. "So you sell yarn."

She laughed. "I also teach knitting and crocheting and embroidery."

"Sorry, I didn't mean to—"

"And I've had one or two men attend my classes."

He looked uncomfortable. "I appreciate you for accepting my apology and not making me learn to knit as payback."

"I wish I'd thought of it. You might have found knitting relaxing." She laughed as she tried to imagine knitting needles in his big calloused hands. "I can't really see you knitting."

He laughed then too, a warm, natural sound that made her soften even more toward him.

"Well, I won't keep you any longer," he said, backing toward the door. Slipping his Stetson back on his head, he tipped his hat to her. "It was nice meeting you, Georgia Michaels."

She smiled and sniffed the bouquet he'd given her as he left, thinking how nice he'd been and wondering what had gone wrong with his marriage to Nicci. They were both gorgeous and both probably rich. But Georgia doubted Nicci had worked a day in her life. Still maybe there was a chance they would reconcile if Nicci stayed around long enough.

Georgia hoped that was possible for Dalton Corbett's sake. He really seemed like a nice man, a man who would take his vows to love, honor and cherish very seriously. Not a man who would ever hurt his wife.

DALTON HOPED he'd handled the situation with Georgia Michaels the right way. If it had been any other woman than the yarn shop owner, he might have tried to persuade her into telling him what had happened to Nicci after he'd left the shop yesterday. He might even have offered a bribe.

But one good look into Georgia Michael's pretty, sweet, girl-next-door face and he knew he would be wasting his time. Kindheartedness radiated from the woman the way greed radiated from other women he'd met.

Even at the threat of death, Georgia Michaels would

cover for another woman who she believed to be in danger. And that, Dalton thought, would be her downfall.

He parked up the street in sight of the shop and now all he could do was wait. If he knew Nicci, which even in their short intense time together, he did, then she would take advantage of a woman like Georgia.

Georgia Michaels was everything Nicci was not, and Nicci would use that to her advantage. Which meant it was just a matter of time before Nicci returned to the yarn shop. She had found a sympathetic woman who'd already helped her. Getting Georgia to help her again would be child's play for a woman like Nicci.

He had to assume from the way Georgia had acted at the shop yesterday that Nicci had brought in an Academy Award winning role as the helpless woman in need. Even if Nicci did return to the shop, he couldn't go in there demanding she talk to him.

Georgia Michaels had already proven she wouldn't hesitate to call the sheriff. Nicci would be counting on that having gained the shop owner's trust.

A little before nine, women began to enter the knitting shop one after another. None of them was Nicci, though. Each woman carried a bag, probably going to one of those classes, Georgia had mentioned. While he had no idea what Nicci had been doing the last nine years, he knew she hadn't taken up knitting.

So how would she ingratiate herself into the shop owner's life and exploit that relationship? Just Georgia Michaels's luck that Nicci had chosen her shop to duck into yesterday. Or had Nicci planned it that way all along?

Dalton grew impatient, anxious to ask Nicci where she'd been all this time and even more to the point what she was doing alive.

Still no sign of Nicci, Dalton started the engine and drove down past the yarn shop. He glanced toward the front window, but the glare of the sun off the glass made it impossible to see inside.

What he did see though stopped his heart cold. Yesterday there'd been an Apartment for Rent sign in the front window. He hadn't noticed it earlier when he'd gone into the shop.

But now there was no mistaking.

The sign was gone.

"AGNES?" Georgia exclaimed when the elderly woman arrived for knitting class.

The last one to come in the door, Agnes stopped and struck a pose. "Like my new 'do? I decided to go à la natural."

"It's cute. I didn't realize you had naturally curly hair."

"Neither did I," Agnes said with a chuckle. "Who knew?"

As Georgia helped her knitting class, she could hear Nicci upstairs moving around. It seemed odd since that apartment had been empty from the time Georgia bought the building and started her shop.

But the sound of life upstairs was also reassuring. She hadn't realized how alone she'd been for some time. It would be nice having someone around—even temporarily.

She was especially anxious for Nicci to come down so she could meet everyone. Georgia wanted Rory to like Nicci and noticed that Rory had been watching the door to the apartments ever since she'd arrived.

"Hello everyone!" Nicci said a few minutes later. She stepped into the class area wearing navy capri pants and a navy-and-white-striped shirt, sandals and the same silver jewelry she'd been wearing the day before.

"Nicci, come join us. I want you to meet my friends."

Georgia introduced them all, doing as Nicci had advised, introducing her by what she had said was her maiden name, Nicci Angeles instead of Corbett.

"That way I won't have to answer a lot of awkward questions," Nicci had said. "You don't mind doing that, do you?"

It was a little white lie of omission. Georgia was happy to do it if it made things easier for Nicci.

As each person was introduced, Nicci complimented the knitting and choice of colors. She especially liked the baby blanket Rory was making and asked when her baby was due.

"The end of the month," Rory said.

"I was thinking Georgia and I should go to a movie tonight at that old fashioned theater I saw in town," Nicci said impulsively. "Rory, I hope you're free and can come with us. I've heard so much about you I feel as if I already know you. Georgia is so lucky to have such a good friend."

AGNES HAD BEEN ANXIOUS to meet the young woman renting the apartment upstairs. She figured Georgia could use the extra income and renting to a young woman close to her own age seemed ideal. Georgia had spoken so highly of the woman this morning before class. Agnes knew she was going to like her.

As Nicci made her way around the class, Agnes began to feel an uncomfortable pressure in her chest. She was suddenly struck by the strangest feeling. Dread. And even more stranger and alien to her, fear.

She felt her smile slip as Nicci now approached her. Why would this slim, attractive young woman fill her with such dread and fear?

Agnes quickly looked down at her knitting, afraid the woman had noticed her reaction, one so foreign to Agnes that she was at a loss to explain it. She was a woman who didn't hold grudges and didn't make enemies and yet—

Nicci stopped in front of her. As Agnes looked up and into the woman's green eyes, she felt a chill rattle through her as if someone had just walked over her grave. For an instant, her gaze locked with the young woman's. Her heart began to pound erratically.

"This is my most faithful knitter," Georgia said by way of introduction. "And," she added lowering her voice, "my favorite."

"I heard *that*," Rory said and everyone laughed.

"This is Agnes Palmer. Meet Nicci Angeles, my new tenant."

"And new *friend*," Nicci added as she reached for Agnes's hand, flinching a little as their fingers touched, her gaze also startled as their eyes locked once again.

Agnes would remember little after that. The moment her fingers touched Nicci's hand, she could recall only the woman's bloodless touch, the soft jingle of the silver bracelets, the murmur of voices around her and the feeling of being out of her body.

Images flashed behind her eyes. A boat rocking in rough seas. Angry voices. Blood. She pulled back her hand as quickly as she could and saw something ugly flicker across the woman's face.

"It is *very* nice to meet you, Agnes," Nicci said, her green eyes as cold as her touch. "I can see why you are such a special student to Georgia. I'm sure we'll be seeing each other again soon."

Agnes heard what she knew was a threat and shuddered inwardly as she forced a smile and murmured, "Nice to meet—" The lie stuck in her throat.

Her fingers, as if of their own accord, began knitting

again. She put a smile on her face and pretended to listen to the others, thankful only when the renter excused herself and left them alone.

Only then did Agnes feel as if she could breathe.

"WELL?" GEORGIA ASKED when she and Rory were alone after the class. "You liked her, didn't you?"

"I saw her for only a few minutes," Rory said noncommittally.

Georgia couldn't hide her disappointment. "I thought for sure the two of you would hit it off."

Rory touched her friend's arm. "I have to be truthful with you, Georgia. There is something about her I don't trust. Did you see the way she got you to go to the show with her tonight by putting you on the spot in front of us all?"

"Come on, it was just a spur-of-the-moment invite."

"You don't know anything about her and she's living across the hall from you and for all you know she could be dangerous."

Georgia groaned. "I'm pretty sure she's not an ax murderer since I helped her unpack and didn't see an ax."

"But you don't know that for sure. It might be one of those folding axes," Rory joked, clearing the air a little. "Seriously, there's something about her. She makes me uneasy."

"I think you're jealous," Georgia said. "And I think it's ridiculous. You're still my best friend."

"*Jealous?*" Rory started to protest then sighed. "Okay, maybe I'm a little jealous, all right? I miss you and this pregnancy makes me a little weird…" She laid a hand on her swollen belly. "But Georgia, I'm not the only one who doesn't trust her. I saw Agnes's reaction to Nicci."

"Oh, please, Agnes likes everyone."

"Exactly. Agnes didn't like her. And I saw Nicci's face

when she shook Agnes's hand. She didn't like Agnes either. It was spooky." Rory shivered. "Agnes almost looked afraid of her."

Georgia laughed. "Do you hear yourself?"

"I know. I sound crazy," Rory admitted. "But look at the way this woman has insinuated herself into your life."

"If this is about the movie tonight, come with us," Georgia said. "You can spend some time around her and see if you still feel the same way."

"I'll think about it."

A horn honked in front of the shop. Georgia waved to Rory's husband. "She'll be right out!" she called to Devlin.

Rory took both of her friend's hands in hers, drawing her attention back. "Honey, just be careful. Promise me you'll try to find out more about her."

Georgia nodded and gave her a hug and then stood back and watched her leave. Maybe Rory was right. What did she really know about Nicci Angeles Corbett?

As she turned, she was startled to find Nicci standing at the back of the shop. From the look on her face, she'd heard *everything*.

Chapter Four

Dalton pulled over once he was around the block from the knitting shop. He tried to convince himself that Nicci wouldn't have rented an apartment in the shop where he'd seen her yesterday for fear he'd come back.

But he knew that's exactly what Nicci would do—and no doubt *had* because she'd found an ally in Georgia Michaels.

Georgia had no idea what kind of woman she'd taken in. And trying to warn her, he feared would be a waste of time. He could only imagine what Nicci had told the shop owner to get Georgia to lie and cover for her.

Dalton knew he had two choices. He could wait around until Nicci decided to let him in on what she was up to. Or he could stir the pot. He wasn't good at sitting around waiting for the other shoe to drop.

He hadn't paid any attention to what kind of vehicle she'd been driving when he thought he'd seen her the other day. But with the closest airport three hours away, that meant she had a rental car parked around here somewhere.

Whitehorse consisted of only a ten-block square, so finding the car shouldn't be that difficult. Even if it didn't have a rental sticker or plate, he should be able to spot it in a town that was ninety-percent pickups.

He took off on foot, determined he would cover the entire town if that's what it took.

His cell phone vibrated.

"So what's going on?" Lantry wanted to know.

Dalton filled him in as he widened his search for Nicci's rental car.

"You gave the woman who owns the yarn shop flowers and apologized to her?" Lantry said, scoffing. "If you suspect this woman lied to you yesterday and is harboring Nicci, why the hell didn't you call her on it? I thought you went into town to find Nicci and demand to know what she wanted."

"You don't know anything about women, do you?" Dalton said.

"Excuse me? I didn't marry *evil incarnate,*" Lantry snapped.

"*I* did, and thanks to Nicci I was provided with a lifetime of learning in a very short while." Ahead, he noticed a nondescript white car. Most people in isolated parts of Montana didn't buy white cars. A white car in a blizzard was dangerous. If you went off the road in a blizzard, white cars weren't easy to spot and you could be stranded for days down a snow-filled gully.

"Not all women are like Nicci."

"Exactly," Dalton agreed. "Georgia Michaels for one. That's why she didn't rat Nicci out yesterday. I'm sure that's also why she would rent the apartment to Nicci. She feels sorry for her and wants to help her."

"Okay, but wouldn't it have made more sense to lay your cards on the table and tell her the truth?"

Dalton chuckled at that. His own brother wasn't going to like the truth when he finally heard it. A complete stranger, a woman who saved other women in distress? Yeah, sure.

"I can imagine how that would have gone over," he

said. "How are you coming on getting the information you need to file for the divorce?"

"I'm trying to get a copy of your marriage license. You're sure you were married in Galveston?"

Dalton frowned. "I assumed so." Was there a chance Nicci had lied about that, too? Maybe the marriage license she'd showed him was a fake. He should be so lucky.

"Nicci Angeles, right? She couldn't have used another name?"

"She showed me a copy of the marriage license the next morning, but truthfully, I didn't notice what name she used."

"She really did drug you?"

"Oh, yeah. She said I drank too much and that's why I couldn't remember getting married. I believed her until I discovered the drug she used on me."

Lantry swore. "What the hell kind of woman did you get tangled up with?"

"A very dangerous one as it turned out."

"I WASN'T EAVESDROPPING, I forgot my purse." Nicci walked over to the counter, picked up a white leather bag and swung it over her shoulder.

"I hope you didn't—"

"Your friend Rory is right," Nicci said, smiling ruefully. "You *don't* know me. Maybe we did become friends too quickly. I have a tendency to come on a little too strong when I really like someone. I'm big on first impressions, but sometimes I'm wrong about a person." She shrugged. "If you want to cancel the show tonight…"

"No," Georgia said. "Rory's been my best friend since we were kids. I think she's feeling a little left out, that's all."

"Well I can understand that. And being pregnant, I'm sure she feels vulnerable as well." Nicci smiled. "I enjoyed meeting your class and your friend Rory. You wait, we're all going to be great friends. I need to run a few errands. Can I get you anything while I'm out?"

"No, but thank you. And thank you for being so understanding about Rory."

"No problem. I know how friends are," Nicci said with a laugh. "See you later."

Georgia tried to work. She'd hoped to get it done before the movie tonight with Nicci. But she couldn't forget what Rory had said about her renter. Nor forget how nice Nicci had been about it. The woman was so gracious.

It was Rory's pregnancy and jealousy, that was all. It made her imagine things. Like Agnes's alleged adverse reaction to Nicci. Why would Agnes of all people dislike Nicci, let alone be afraid of her?

Georgia knew she wouldn't be able to get any work done until she talked to Rory.

"WHY DO I get the feeling there's more to the story?" Lantry said on the other end of the line.

"Because you're my brother. I have to go." Dalton hung up as he reached the white car and glanced inside. Too clean for this part of Montana where there were more dirt roads than paved. Dust boiled up miles away in the summer, letting residents see if someone was coming long before they arrived.

If he was right, this was Nicci's rental car. It wasn't as if there were a bunch of rental cars in Whitehorse. He hesitated, considering why Nicci hadn't gone with an expensive one. She'd gone cheap and nondescript. That alone made him suspicious.

Maybe Lantry was right. Maybe she was broke and that's what this was about. Or maybe she just hadn't wanted to stand out. Which in itself was amusing since the woman herself would have a hell of a time blending into a crowd— let alone blending in with the locals in Whitehorse.

A thought hit him like a brick to the forehead. If Nicci had come here to end things, she hadn't come alone. She would have brought Ambrose.

Dalton scanned the nearly empty street as he thought of the name he'd heard Nicci screaming that night on the boat. *Kill him, Ambrose, kill him!*

Ambrose was no doubt the same man he'd caught her talking to that day on her cell phone at the hotel before they set sail. He'd definitely been in the large motorboat Dalton had seen following them.

Dalton still couldn't believe how stupid he'd been and now he had no doubt that Nicci had brought Ambrose with her to Whitehorse. Unfortunately, Dalton hadn't gotten a good look at Ambrose that night at sea. But he'd bet money the guy would stand out in Whitehorse—just as Nicci had. So where was she hiding him until she needed him?

He shuddered at the thought. Ambrose did whatever Nicci told him to do apparently. Even commit murder for her.

Dalton considered what it would take to bring Ambrose out of hiding. He needed to know what he was up against.

Glancing around, he pulled out his pocket knife, then bent down and stuck the blade into the rear tire. Then he did the same thing to the front tire before walking back to his pickup to wait.

The only way to deal with Nicci was to play dirty. The problem was Nicci played till the death.

"ARE YOU ALL RIGHT?" Rory asked when Georgia called her. "You sound funny."

Georgia was hesitant to talk to Rory about Nicci's

personal life, but she really needed her best friend right now. "I want to tell you something but you have to keep it to yourself."

"You know I won't tell anyone."

"The reason Nicci is in town is because she's here to get a divorce from Dalton Corbett."

"Dalton Corbett and Nicci? I don't believe it."

"Well, it's true. *That's* how I met Nicci. She was standing in front of the shop looking at the Apartment for Rent sign and must have seen Dalton. She ducked in here and he chased her into the shop and was very upset when he didn't find her."

"You *hid* her?"

"No. Not exactly. She dropped down behind some boxes from my yarn delivery that morning," Georgia said. "But I did fib when he asked me if I knew where she went. You should have seen her. She was shaking she was so frightened of him."

"That's terrible," Rory said sympathetically.

"She needed somewhere to stay until she gets the divorce taken care of and she loved the apartment, so I rented it to her. If you think it was impulsive, it was."

"I would have done the same thing under the circumstances," Rory said, making her feel better.

"Dalton Corbett came into the shop this morning to apologize. He brought me roses. I have to admit, I felt sorry for him. If you had seen how upset he was yesterday. Clearly he's still in love with her."

"Where is Nicci now?"

"She said she had to run a few errands. I'm worried that she might have gone out to the ranch. She says she just wants to work out an amicable divorce."

"When I met her, I felt like she was hiding something,"

Rory said. "Now I feel bad about what I said about her. If the offer is still open, I would like to go to the movie with you and Nicci."

"Of course it is," Georgia said, glad she'd told Rory the truth and relieved since she trusted Rory's judgment. Rory's misgivings about Nicci had worried her. Agnes's reaction to Nicci still worried her and she said as much to Rory.

"Agnes seems pretty perceptive when it comes to people," Rory said. "I swear she looked scared when she met Nicci. But maybe I was wrong."

Georgia shivered as a bad feeling washed over her. "What if Agnes's fear wasn't for herself but for Nicci? You don't think Dalton would harm her, do you?"

DALTON HAD PARKED his pickup under the limbs of a large poplar tree where he had a clear view of the rental car. He called Lantry back.

"You are aware, I assume, that it's against the law to slash someone's tires?" Lantry asked sarcastically. "This woman does bring out the worst in you, doesn't she?"

"You have no idea."

Dalton had gotten into more trouble in his younger years than any of his brothers. Not even Lantry knew how much trouble. Only their father and his high-priced lawyers who had saved Dalton's neck more times than he could count knew the extent of it.

That's why he'd kept the mess with Nicci to himself. He had been bound and determined to get himself out of it. One way or the other.

He felt the same way now. Older and wiser, he hoped he wasn't playing right into Nicci's hands. Look where it had gotten him last time.

He watched the rental car, ready if it turned out not to

be Nicci's. He'd make it up to the stranger—and then some. But if there was a chance of drawing Ambrose out…

Dalton was starting to think this might have been a fool's errand when Nicci came around the corner and started down the street toward the rental car—and him.

He hunkered down in the pickup seat as Nicci glanced around as she neared the car. She was looking for him. Expecting to see him. He couldn't see her expression from this distance, but he would bet she was smiling.

She slowed, then stopped abruptly, no doubt spotting the two flat tires.

Her gaze shot up, aimed down the street, her body language rigid with anger. He didn't move. Where he was parked under the poplar trees, the shadows from the overhanging limbs making patterns on the pickup's windshield, he was sure she couldn't see him.

But she would know who'd done the damage. Would she also know that he'd stick around to see her reaction?

Nicci glanced once more at the tires, then hands on her hips and head up, she looked down the street again, her stance challenging. Oh, she knew, all right.

He almost got out to confront her. But if there was a chance of drawing out Ambrose, he had to take it. Turning, she walked back up the block. His question as to whether or not she would call Ambrose for help was quickly answered when Nicci returned a few minutes before a tow truck showed up.

But this time, his attention was on the woman with her. Georgia Michaels. Unlike Nicci, who was dressed as if going to the beach, Georgia wore jeans, boots and a Western shirt. The two couldn't have looked more different.

Even from this distance he could see that Georgia was upset—just as Nicci had wanted him to see. Nicci put a

comforting arm around her new ally as the tow truck took
the car down to the tire shop and the two women walked
back down the street.

Dalton swore. He'd failed to flush out Ambrose, but
worse, Nicci had used the incident to garner even more of
Georgia's sympathy and make him look even more dangerous, he thought as he saw Georgia give Nicci a set of keys.

Nicci glanced back. Without even seeing her expression, he knew there was a look of triumph on her face.

WHEN SOMETHING was worrying Agnes, she headed for her
garden. The hailstorm had played havoc with her crop.
Testing the ground between her rows of tomato plants and
finding it dried by the morning sun, she knelt, hoping to
find her usual sense of peace out here.

A breeze teased the leaves of the tree where she'd put
her tubs of tomatoes just yesterday. Determined not to
think about anything negative, Agnes sat counting her
blessings. She had so much to be thankful for, she thought,
as she breathed in the familiar scents of her garden.

After a few moments she went to work, pulling weeds,
picking blossoms from the tomatoes that didn't stand a
chance of bearing fruit and checking her other plants to see
how much damage was done by the storm.

As hard as she tried to keep her thoughts from circling
back to Georgia and that woman renting her spare apartment, Agnes failed. Her run-in with Nicci had taken a lot
out of her. She thought about quitting knitting class.

"No," Agnes said out loud with a shake of her head. She
couldn't abandon Georgia. Georgia was going to need her.
"Now how do I know that?" she asked herself, frowning.
Ever since yesterday, she'd been getting the strangest
notions in her head.

Agnes turned at the sound of a vehicle coming up the road. Being slight in stature, she could barely see over the top of the tomato plant where she knelt. She peered through the plants and saw Georgia's pickup turn into the yard and park next to her car.

Alarms went off as Agnes realized that Georgia had never been out to the house before. Something must be wrong.

Starting to rise, she quickly dropped back down when the truck door opened and she saw who stepped out. Not Georgia.

She ducked her snow-white, curly head behind one of her taller tomato plants. Her heart pounded fiercely in her chest and her hands trembled as she watched Georgia's renter walk toward the front of the house.

Nicci glanced around as she mounted the steps to the porch. She had something in her hand, a small white box like those from the local bakery.

Agnes stayed put, listening to Nicci knock on the front door. Silence, then another knock, this one harder. Peeking out, she saw Nicci glance toward Agnes's car parked out front, then knock again.

Anticipating Nicci's next move, Agnes crawled deeper into the garden until she'd put the wide trunk of the oak tree between her and the house.

Nicci's sandal heels tapped across the porch to the garden side. Agnes could imagine her leaning over the railing looking in this direction. She held her breath and silently wished the woman away.

Tap. Tap. Tap. The porch steps creaked. If Nicci came out into the garden… Moments passed. The pickup door opened, then closed. The engine revved, gravel crunched under the tires.

Agnes stayed hidden, heart pounding with fear, as

she listened to the sound of the pickup engine die off in the distance.

She stayed hidden until the dust had settled on the road. Only then did she rise and make her way back to the house.

The small white bakery box sat on the front step where Nicci had left it.

Agnes picked it up, opening it carefully. The words *Have a Nice Day!* were printed in icing on an oversize cupcake.

A dozen thoughts raced through her mind as she stared down at the gift. How had Nicci found her house out here in the country? Why, all she had to do was ask someone in town. Still it seemed odd that Nicci would go to the trouble.

And why come all this way out here to deliver a cupcake when there was no doubt that Nicci knew how Agnes felt about her? Had Nicci singled her out or given cupcakes to everyone from the class she'd met that morning?

It irritated Agnes.

Worse, it made her feel terrible because she still had such negative thoughts about the woman. Maybe that had been the point of the cupcake.

Feeling guilty, she carried the small box around the house and tossed it into the fifty-five-gallon barrel she used to burn her refuse. As she started to step away, shocked at herself for such ungrateful behavior, she heard a noise and turned to see three of those pesky trash birds had landed on the rim of the barrel. Others were already sweeping down to attack the cupcake with relish.

At least the cupcake hadn't gone to waste, Agnes thought as she went back into the house to make herself some lunch. She was washing up the few dishes she'd dirtied when she looked out in the backyard and saw one of the birds from earlier. It lay on its side in the dirt next to the trash barrel.

Drying her hands, she stepped out the back door. The afternoon felt too quiet. The hair on her neck stood on end as she neared the barrel. Where were the other birds?

She peered into the barrel. "Oh, my heavens!" she cried with a gasp as she stumbled back.

A dozen scavenger birds lay dead in the bottom of the barrel next to the empty cupcake box.

Chapter Five

Georgia was closing up the shop for the day when she heard Nicci return in tears.

"What is it?" she asked, locking the front door behind her. She'd been worried all afternoon about her, suspecting she'd been planning to go out to the Trails West Ranch. "Dalton didn't try to hurt you, did he?"

"I'm sorry, I don't want to burden you with my problems. You've already been so kind to me," Nicci said between tears.

"Let's go up to my apartment," Georgia said, seeing how upset Nicci was. "I could make us some tea or I have some wine."

"Wine," Nicci said, between sniffs as they started up the stairs. "Definitely wine."

Once inside the apartment, Georgia poured them each a glass, then took a seat across from Nicci in the small living room.

"I love what you did with your apartment," Nicci said, wiping her tears.

"Thank you. Now tell me what's wrong."

Nicci took a sip of her wine and closed her eyes. "Oh, I needed this." She put down her glass and sighed as if making up her mind. "I promised myself I wouldn't involve you in this," she said resolutely, and dried an errant tear before plastering on a smile.

"We're friends. You can talk to me. I know you're going through a hard time now."

Nicci's eyes filled. "You are so kind and caring. I'm not used to that. The truth is I've never had any really close girlfriends."

"Did you see Dalton?" Georgia asked.

Nicci shook her head. "I couldn't even get near the ranch. I thought that if I could get the divorce papers into his hands…"

Georgia wished she'd known. She could have given the papers to Dalton when he was in the shop earlier that morning. She hadn't mentioned his visit to Nicci, not wanting to upset her. It was also the reason she'd brought the bouquet of roses he'd given her up to her apartment rather than put them in a vase in the shop.

Dalton had said he would do anything for Georgia if she'd accept his apology. Wouldn't he have been surprised if she had handed him divorce papers?

"Now I don't know what I'm going to do," Nicci said. "I foolishly thought that he might just sign them and give them back and it would be over."

"He must still love you," Georgia said. "Are you sure there is no chance for your marriage?"

"*None*. He might have loved me, but he doesn't now."

"How can you be so sure?"

Nicci smiled. "I know." She took another sip of her wine. "I guess I'll be forced to have him served, which will make him angry, then he'll drag this whole thing out much longer than I hoped."

"I could give them to him," Georgia heard herself say.

Nicci looked up. "No. That would mean you'd have to drive out to his ranch. I wouldn't ask you to do that."

"I wouldn't mind. I know how important this is to you." Georgia couldn't help herself. She wanted to help even though it would mean that Nicci would be leaving town sooner.

Nicci leaned over to give Georgia a hug. "Dalton wants this divorce as badly as I do. He's just being difficult because of his huge ego. Maybe he'll even sign the papers while you're there."

"I can take them out there now and be back in time for the movie. I'll just give Rory a call and let her know what the plan is."

"Rory's going to the movie with us?" Nicci asked, sounding surprised.

Georgia nodded, smiling. "I hope you don't mind."

"Of course not. I'm glad she changed her mind." Nicci downed her wine and went next door to her apartment. She returned a few moments later with a large manila envelope and a small white box tied with a red ribbon.

"Just give him this," she said, handing Georgia the manila envelope. "You don't even have to talk to him. Knowing Dalton, he won't open the envelope while you're there so don't worry about trying to get him to sign them. That was just wishful thinking on my part."

"Okay. Don't worry. It will be fine."

Nicci smiled broadly. "I know. That's why this is for you." She thrust the small white box at her.

Georgia was already shaking her head.

"It's just a small token of my gratitude," Nicci said. "*Please.* I feel badly about all this as it is. You have to take the present."

She had no choice. She took the small box. Nicci

watched with obvious excited anticipation as Georgia untied the ribbon and opened the lid and let out a surprised breath. She lifted out the silver hoops.

"They're beautiful, but—"

"They reminded me of you," Nicci said. "Put them on. They'll go great with your haircut."

Georgia removed the small studs she was wearing and put on the silver hoops.

"Here, look," Nicci said, drawing her over to the mirror on the wall.

Georgia felt uncomfortable taking the gift but could see how pleased Nicci was. "They're beautiful. Thank you."

"*You're* beautiful and such a great friend," Nicci said with almost an embarrassed laugh. "You've done so much for me. I can never repay you."

DALTON CORBETT watched dust boil up on the road and roll into the ranch. After the tire incident, he'd been expecting company. He waited, standing on the front porch of his cabin, planning to head off the driver. He wasn't going to let Nicci get to the rest of his family if he could damn well prevent it.

As the vehicle approached though, he was surprised to see that it wasn't the white rental car he'd been anticipating.

Nor was the driver behind the wheel Nicci. Or a man who might have been Ambrose.

He cursed as he saw that it was Georgia Michaels, the owner of the yarn shop.

The pickup slowed to stop as he stepped off the porch and into the dirt road. Dust settled slowly in the hot summer evening air.

As Georgia climbed out of the pickup, he saw that she held a large manila envelope in her hand and looked all business as she walked toward him.

"Nicci asked me to give this to you," she said, holding it out.

He glanced at the envelope, wondering if this woman had any idea what she had become involved in. "What is it?"

She swallowed, clearly uncomfortable in the position Nicci had put her in. "Divorce papers."

He laughed. "I wouldn't bet on that. I'm sorry Nicci's got you doing her dirty work now." He shook his head in disgust, though not surprised. Hadn't he known Nicci would use her? Georgia Michaels was an easy mark—decent, trusting, caring.

"Please just take the envelope," she said.

Something was different about her. It took him a moment to realize what. The large silver hoops at her ears. Hadn't he noticed small pearl stubs in her ears when he'd stopped by her shop with the flowers?

"New earrings?"

Guiltily, Georgia's hand went to one of the large hoops. In a flash, he knew. His stomach clenched. The silver hoops had been a present from Nicci—a bribe.

"Step out of the heat for a moment," he said and, without waiting for a response, went back up on the porch and took a chair. He was shaking inside, furious with Nicci for drawing this woman into this. But he couldn't let Georgia leave without at least trying to warn her.

She stood in the hot afternoon sun for a moment, then joined him on the porch, perching on the edge of the other rocker. "I really need to get back."

"Why didn't Nicci bring this out herself?"

"She did. She said she couldn't get onto the ranch."

He glanced at the open road. "You didn't have any trouble getting on the ranch, did you?"

A flicker of doubt crossed her pretty face. The woman

was so incredibly open, radiating honesty and integrity. She was a sitting duck for a woman like Nicci.

"Did Nicci tell you that our marriage didn't last a week, that I haven't seen or spoken to her in nine years, that I thought she was dead until I saw her in front of your shop?" He nodded at Georgia's shocked expression. "I didn't think so. That's why I was so upset yesterday when I burst into your shop. I thought I'd seen a ghost."

Georgia would have made a terrible poker player. Her face registered shock, then guilt at her part in hiding in Nicci yesterday. "If you don't want a divorce—"

"Is that what she told you? That I won't give her a divorce?" Dalton felt his temper rising, but one look at Georgia's face and he put a damper on it.

Lowering his voice, he said, "There is nothing I would like more than a divorce from Nicci." He shook his head. "You have to understand, Nicci doesn't let go of something until she's destroyed it."

"I really don't want to get in the middle of this," Georgia said, rising.

He met her gaze. Her eyes were a rich brown with flecks of gold, like treasure behind her long lashes. "You *are* in the middle," he said. "That's what I'm trying to tell you. You're right where Nicci wants you or you wouldn't be here now. If she really wanted a divorce, wouldn't she have contacted me the moment she got into town? And why wait nine years? I haven't heard from her and she sure as hell hasn't been out here to the ranch."

Georgia's face closed and he saw that he'd gone too far.

"Look, I'm sorry. I don't know how you got in the middle of this… Yes, I do. Nicci needs you. What worries me is what happens when she's done with you. Or if you do something to turn her against you. You have no idea what's moved in on you—and not just into your house. The woman is dangerous. More dangerous than you can imagine."

"Under the circumstances—"

"That's just it, you don't *know* the circumstances," he interrupted. "All you know is what *she's* told you."

"You *cut* her tires."

He leaned back, ashamed, and nodded slowly. He almost added, "Yeah, well, *she* tried to cut my throat," but he caught himself.

"I SHOULDN'T HAVE said that," Georgia cried, regretting accusing him the instant the words had left her mouth. This was none of her business and she started to say as much when he cut her off.

"I shouldn't have cut her tires. I was desperate. I hoped it would force her to contact me. I have no way to contact her, to find out what happened nine years ago, to find out what she wants after all this time."

"Well, I think you accomplished what you wanted." Georgia held out the envelope again. "She says she wants a divorce."

Georgia just wanted to leave. The man confused her. She didn't know who to believe. But seeing the pain in his handsome face, hearing it in his voice, she believed *him*.

"Please take this. I feel very uncomfortable being put in this position."

He nodded. "I'm sorry that happened." His gaze locked with hers for a long moment before he took the envelope.

"I just did Nicci a one-time favor. That's all." Georgia turned to leave.

"That's what I'm trying to tell you. This won't be all, trust me. She's already got you lying for her, hiding her, running her nasty errands. Do *yourself* a favor. Shake her loose before you regret it. If you're lucky the most she'll do is use you. But if you cross her…"

Georgia walked to her pickup, climbed in and closed the door on the rest of his words. As she drove off the Trails West Ranch, she felt shaken after her encounter with Dalton Corbett.

She hated that she'd let Nicci talk her into bringing out the divorce papers. What was she saying? She'd *volunteered*. But what choice did she have, given how upset Nicci had been?

This was all her own fault. Hadn't she been leery about renting the apartment to a woman in the middle of a divorce? And yet she had. Same with coming out here today.

Georgia vowed she wouldn't make that mistake again. She would let Nicci and Dalton handle this from here on out.

But as she drove toward town, Dalton's words haunted her. Nicci had said she hadn't been allowed on the ranch. But Georgia had had no trouble, just as Dalton had pointed out.

The shocker had been what he'd said about their marriage. Could it be true that he hadn't seen Nicci for nine years? Why had he thought she was dead? If their marriage hadn't lasted a week, did that mean there had been an accident on their honeymoon?

She recalled how upset he'd been the other day at the shop when he'd come in looking for Nicci. His actions made sense now. But why had Nicci acted afraid of him? To hear Dalton tell it—only to get Georgia to cover for her.

Well, had that been the case, it had worked like a charm.

No, Georgia thought, remembering the way Nicci had been trembling after Dalton left. She *was* afraid of him and there had to be a reason. The man had cut the tires on Nicci's rental car! Who knew what he'd done on their honeymoon?

Georgia put it out of her mind. It wasn't any of her business. Dalton had the divorce papers. It was out of her hands.

She glanced at her watch. She was just going to make it back in time for the movie at eight. She had called Rory on the way out to Trails West Ranch and told her to meet them at the movie rather than at the apartment since she hadn't been sure she'd get back in time.

She'd also promised to call Nicci as soon as she'd delivered the papers. She wasn't looking forward to it, wanting to put the whole uncomfortable experience behind her. But dutifully, she placed the call.

"I gave him the papers," she said when Nicci answered her cell.

"What did he say?"

Georgia was a little taken aback by the question. "Nothing."

"Did he open the envelope?"

"No, not while I was there. I'm on my way into town," she said, just wanting to change the subject. "Rory is meeting us at the theater."

"Come on, he didn't even try to tell you his side of things?" Nicci asked.

"I'm sure he felt it was none of my business." She waited for Nicci to say something, fighting the feeling that Nicci was angry with her and knew she wasn't telling the truth. Dalton was right about at least one thing. Since Nicci had come into her life, she had taken up lying.

When Nicci still said nothing, Georgia said, "See you soon." She clicked off, grateful they were going to the movie tonight. She feared otherwise Nicci might want to grill her half the night.

On impulse, Georgia called Rory.

"I'm on my way," Rory said, sounding rushed. "Honestly. Just headin' out the door."

Georgia laughed. "I didn't call to nag you, although you know I hate missing the previews."

"Don't worry, I'll be there before the previews begin. How did your errand go?"

"I delivered the papers."

"He didn't put up a fight?"

"Not much of one, no. He did tell me the marriage didn't even last a week, that he hasn't seen her in nine years and thought she was dead."

"You have to be kidding!"

"Nope."

"No wonder he was so upset yesterday at your shop. Of course he might not be telling the truth."

"I believe him. If you could have seen his face…"

"You think he still loves her?"

"Rory, always the romantic," Georgia joked. "If he still loves her, he does a good job of hiding it. He admitted he cut the tires on her rental car. He said he was desperate for her to contact him."

Georgia heard a pickup door slam and an engine turn over on the other end of the line. Rory was on her way into town.

"Wait a minute," Rory said. "If he was so desperate to talk to her… This doesn't make sense. I thought the only reason you had to take the papers out was because he wouldn't let Nicci on the ranch."

Georgia took a breath and let it out slowly. "I think she might have lied about that," she said, touching one of the silver hoop earrings now dangling from her lobes. Clearly Nicci had known all along that she could talk Georgia into taking the divorce papers out to Dalton. That's why she had the present wrapped and ready.

She said as much to Rory. "I think she might have played me."

"You think?"

DALTON SAT for a long time on the porch. Not even the breeze coming off the prairie was cool this evening. He'd tossed the manila envelope on the chair next to him. He knew he should open it and see what surprise Nicci had in store for him.

It sure as hell wasn't divorce papers, he'd bet the ranch on that. A woman who wanted a divorce didn't go about it this way.

What had him upset right now was the way he'd handled things with Georgia Michaels. He'd lost his temper and said things that had upset her. But he couldn't stand the thought that Nicci was using this nice young woman. He should have just taken the damned envelope and saved his breath.

But he'd felt he had to warn Georgia. Unfortunately, Nicci had already gotten to her and he knew only too well how persuasive Nicci could be when she wanted something. Whatever she wanted now, she had Georgia doing her bidding.

Angrily, he reached over and snatched up the envelope, ripping it open and dumping the contents onto the chair next to him.

A stack of blank sheets of white paper fluttered out. He stared at the pile, thinking that couldn't be all. What was this? Just a test to see if she could get Georgia to do her bidding? Nicci had lied to Georgia to make her believe she was delivering some kind of legal documents, so why was Dalton surprised?

But his instincts told him there had to be more to it.

He picked up the stack of blank sheets, thumbed through them to see if any of the pages had writing on them. A half dozen photographs fell to the floor, landing faceup.

One glance at the top photo and he knew exactly when they all were taken. Although the photographs were grainy, taken at night, there was no doubt.

He was staring down at an attempted murder—recorded on film. But what struck him wasn't the horror of what the camera had captured, but the full knowledge of what Nicci had hoped to accomplish that night on the sailboat out at sea.

She wanted to see how far he would go. She'd set it up so she not only pushed him to the point of murder and engineered an escape plan for herself and Ambrose, but she also had the photographs as evidence.

So why had she waited nine years?

And how far was she planning to go this time?

GEORGIA FOUND HERSELF dreading the end of the movie. Nicci hadn't been herself all night. Earlier she'd been waiting at the apartment, clearly anxious. No, not anxious, excited. Her eyes had been bright and she seemed too wound up, like someone who had drunk too much caffeine.

"Are you going to tell me what he had to say?" were the first words out of her mouth.

"I already told you," Georgia said, glancing at her watch. "We have to go. Rory will be waiting at the theater for us."

"I know Dalton. He told you his side," Nicci said as they walked the two blocks to the theater. "So the fact that you won't tell me what he said must mean you believe him."

"I already told you—"

"Let's just forget it. I'm sorry I asked."

Georgia had been glad to see Rory's pickup parked out front and a very pregnant Rory standing next to it. They'd talked for a few minutes in front of the theater, but Nicci had been clearly distracted.

Once inside, Georgia and Rory had to have a large container of buttered popcorn, candy and a soda before they were seated in the middle of the huge, nearly empty theater for the chick flick that was playing. Nicci hadn't wanted anything to eat or drink.

Georgia had been determined to enjoy herself. It had been so long since she and Rory had done this. She ignored how quiet Nicci was or that she didn't laugh at the funny parts.

"She's getting a divorce, of course she's got other stuff besides a movie on her mind," Rory whispered halfway through the film when Nicci excused herself to go to the bathroom.

Like lying to me about not being able to get on the ranch?

"You're probably right. I'd just hoped we could have fun tonight."

"Well, *I'm* having fun," Rory whispered and reached for another handful of buttered popcorn.

Georgia knew Rory was right. Whatever was bothering Nicci, she was staying out of it. This new distance between her and Nicci was good. Georgia had gotten too close to her renter and that had been a mistake.

After that little pep talk, she lost herself in the movie and barely noticed when Nicci returned.

"YOU'RE GOING to have to tell the family," Lantry said as he climbed the steps to Dalton's cabin.

"So you found a record of the marriage." Dalton felt the full weight of his disappointment. He'd hoped maybe the marriage had been a sham from the beginning, including the legalities. Nicci had lied about so much, why not the marriage? He should have known he couldn't get that lucky.

"I could use a drink," Dalton said, getting up to head into his cabin.

"They're serving drinks over at the main house and holding dinner for us," Lantry said, stopping him. "You can't put this off any longer. It will be better coming from you than having your *wife* show up on our doorstep."

Knowing Nicci, he was a little surprised she hadn't done just that. Instead she was playing some cat-and-mouse game using Georgia Michaels. He feared what her next move would be.

"She isn't here to give you a divorce," Lantry said. "Or the papers would have already been served."

"Don't you think I know that? I just hate to involve the family in this." For all those years when he was young, Dalton had depended on his father to get him out of one scrape after another. That had usually meant throwing money at the problem. Money wasn't going to work this time. "I need to handle this myself."

"Hell, the family is already involved, especially Dad. Maybe this woman *was* rich when you married her, but you can bet the reason it's taken her nine years to look you up again is money."

He didn't bother arguing with his brother. Eventually, he'd have to tell his brother everything. As his lawyer, Lantry would have to know what was at stake.

Dalton got to his feet.

"Where are you going?"

"To tell the family. You want to come?"

"Hell, no." Lantry smiled. "But I will. You'll need all the allies you can get."

They walked over to the main house to find the rest of the family gathered in the great room before supper.

"I wondered where you two had gotten off to," Grayson said congenially from behind the bar. "What can I get you, son?"

"I'm fine," Dalton said.

"I'll take whatever you're having," Lantry said when his father motioned to him. "Just make mine a double."

The others turned then to look at the two of them. Shane was in his usual chair that looked out over the ranch. Jud was at the bar along with Kate. Russell was in a chair reading the latest stockman news. He, too, looked up.

"What's going on?" Grayson asked, handing Lantry a drink.

"I'm married," Dalton said without preamble.

"What?" came the chorus from around the room.

"I got married nine years ago."

"You're *married?*" Jud asked. "What kind of bull is this?"

"It's true. I kept the marriage a secret."

"Why would you do that?" Grayson asked.

Kate had gotten up from where she'd been sitting and walked around to stand next to her husband as if she thought he was going to need her support.

His father made Dalton a drink and pushed it into his hand. "I think you might need this, son."

Dalton took a gulp. It burned all the way down before settling like a ball of fire in his belly. "I just wanted you all to know because…" He hesitated. "She's in town and she might cause trouble."

A groan rose up in the room. Dalton's attention was on his father. Grayson had paled.

"I don't believe it will be about money," Dalton assured him. "She was rich when I married her."

"Sure she was," his older brother Russell said.

"I'm sorry. I know I've disappointed you," Dalton said to his father. He would disappoint him a lot more before this was over, he feared.

"It's all right, son," Grayson said. "Is there is anything I can do?"

"No, but thanks. Lantry is handling the paperwork."

"Wait a minute," his brother Jud said. "For nine years you never said anything about this?"

"The marriage didn't last a week. There was an accident on the honeymoon. I thought she was lost at sea."

"Oh, Dalton, I'm so sorry," Kate said.

He felt like such a jackass accepting sympathy given the part he'd played.

"This must come as a shock for you," Kate said. "Did she say where she's been the last nine years?"

"I haven't talked to her yet."

Grayson frowned. "She's your *wife*. I would think she would contact you when she got to town."

"Maybe she wants to see the lay of the land first," Shane said.

"Shane's right. You could have remarried for all she knows," Kate said.

Not likely, given how his first marriage had gone.

"I suspect she's more interested in finding out what she can get," Russell said.

Kate waved that away. "Dalton, maybe you should delay taking any legal action. If there is a chance of saving your marriage, you don't want to do anything rash."

Saving his marriage? Doing anything rash? This conversation had taken on a surreal quality. They were talking about Nicci as if she were rational and sane, a real wife in a real marriage.

His cell phone vibrated. He checked the caller ID and felt his pulse spike. *Speak of the devil.*

Chapter Six

"Great movie," Rory said as Georgia and Nicci walked her to her pickup parked at the curb outside the theater. "I shouldn't have eaten that popcorn and candy and soda. This baby is going to pop out addicted to junk food."

Georgia laughed. Next to her Nicci chuckled and checked her watch. "I had fun," Georgia said, giving Rory a hug. "I'm glad you came in for the movie."

"Me, too." Rory shifted her gaze to Nicci who was fiddling with her cell phone. "Thanks for inviting me."

"Sure. Any friend of Georgia's is a friend of mine," Nicci said, putting Georgia on guard. Nicci was still angry with her. The walk home was not going to be fun.

"I have to make a call I completely forgot about," Nicci said suddenly. "You don't mind, do you, Georgia?"

"Not at all." She hated that she sounded so relieved.

Rory climbed into her truck and they watched Nicci placing her call as she walked down the street away from them.

"Okay, she's acting weird."

Georgia laughed. "She thinks I'm holding out on her. She wants to know *everything* Dalton said when I delivered the divorce papers. I should never have gotten involved."

"You didn't tell her?"

"No. I don't want her telling Dalton when she sees him 'Georgia said you said…' No," Georgia said, holding up her hand. "I refuse to be in the middle of this."

"Good luck with that." She reached over to touch one of the silver hoops. "Those really are great earrings. They are so…"

"Not me," Georgia said with a laugh.

Rory laughed as well. "They really are more me. After Nicci leaves town—"

"They're all yours," Georgia said. "I am *so* glad you came in for the movie. This was fun."

"It was, but I better get home. Devlin will be calling out the National Guard soon."

They said their goodbyes and Georgia started down the street toward her shop, hoping she could avoid Nicci tonight and feeling guilty for even the thought. She couldn't imagine what Nicci must be going through.

DALTON GLANCED from his cell phone to his family. "If you'll excuse me. I have to take this."

He stepped outside and without preamble said, "I wondered when I'd be hearing from you, Nicci." His voice had a knife edge to it he couldn't help. It felt just like the knife edge Nicci had put to his throat nine years ago.

"That wasn't nice what you did to my car," Nicci said in that soft, seductive tone she pulled out when she wanted something. "You surprise me, Dalton."

"I doubt that." Just the sound of her voice turned his stomach.

She laughed.

"Let's get this over with, Nicci. What do you want?"

The laughter died off. "I thought we should talk."

"I thought we were."

"I prefer talking face-to-face," she said.

"Fine. Where are you? I can leave right now."

"So anxious and after all this time…"

"Let's not forget, I thought you were dead."

"That's right." She laughed again and he heard the tinkle of her silver bracelets. That sound transported him back to that night on the sea and for a moment he heard nothing but the rush of his own blood through his veins.

"Did you hear me?"

He hadn't. "What?"

"I asked what you told Georgia." She let out an irritated sigh. "I warned her that you would tell her a bunch of lies."

So Georgia hadn't told her about their talk. "Why would I tell her anything? She has nothing to do with this. I just took the nasty little present you made her deliver and sent her on her way." Did she believe him?

"You have always been so transparent, Dalton," Nicci said.

"Apparently so."

"Do you want to meet me or not?"

Not. "Why even ask? You know the answer or you wouldn't have called."

He could hear the smile in her voice as she said, "Tomorrow then."

"What's wrong with tonight?" His free hand clenched into a fist at the thought of wrapping his hands around her throat.

"I have plans. I'll call you in the morning and set up a time and place. Until then…"

He heard her disconnect and stood for a moment, listening to his pulse coursing through his veins. He'd been so furious with Nicci that he'd almost missed the fact that she was mad as hell.

But at whom? Him? Or Georgia? Fear burrowed under his skin. Georgia hadn't confided in Nicci about what he'd said to her when she'd come out to the ranch. Nicci would take that as a betrayal.

"Oh, hell," he said, and thought about calling Georgia. And saying what? He'd already warned her about Nicci. She'd made it perfectly clear she didn't want to hear anymore.

Well, Georgia was about to find out what happened when she crossed Nicci for the first time.

"Nicci, right?"

Dalton turned to find his brother Lantry leaning against one of the porch posts. He hadn't heard him come out. "Yeah, she wants to meet face-to-face."

"Tonight?"

"Tomorrow."

"Are you sure that's a good idea?"

Dalton laughed. Lantry had no idea how bad an idea it was. "How else am I going to find out what she wants and put an end to this?" He felt as if a clock was ticking, as much for Georgia Michaels as it was for himself.

GEORGIA OPENED the back door of the shop as quietly as possible and slipped in, not bothering to turn on a light. If she was lucky she could get up to her apartment without—

"You don't have to sneak," Nicci said from the darkness.

Georgia jumped, her hand going to her mouth to keep from crying out. She'd so hoped Nicci was up in her apartment.

Instead, her renter rose from one of the chairs used for knitting classes and walked toward her from out of the deep shadow of the shop. With a shiver, Georgia realized Nicci had been sitting in the dark waiting for her.

"I didn't mean to scare you," Nicci said, but Georgia

doubted that. "It was just so peaceful in here, I didn't even want to turn on a light." Her voice softened. "I was starting to worry about you."

"You shouldn't have. I thought you'd already gone up," Georgia managed to say. She had desperately wished that was the case, but hoped it hadn't come out in her tone. Nicci was angry enough at her already without making things worse.

"I was waiting for you. If I hadn't had to make that darned call… I thought we could have a glass of wine and talk about the movie."

"It's late and I have to work early in the morning," Georgia said, sensing that turning Nicci down wasn't her best move. But she had to put some distance between her and her renter. And she knew what would happen. Nicci would get back on the topic of Dalton and Georgia's conversation with him.

"The truth is I wanted to apologize. I shouldn't have asked you to take those papers out to Dalton." Nicci held up a hand to stop Georgia from speaking although Georgia hadn't opened her mouth. "Then when you came back I gave you the third degree. I'm sorry. You're my friend and I've put you in a terrible position."

"It's all right. It's over. Let's just forget it." Georgia turned toward the stairs, wanting only to escape.

"I'm glad you feel that way. Rory seemed to enjoy the movie," Nicci said as she followed Georgia up the stairs. "So you two have known each other since Mrs. Michaels adopted you?"

Georgia had forgotten she'd told Nicci about that. It wasn't something most people in Whitehorse knew. She regretted confiding in Nicci now, feeling as if her renter was trying to use it to either get closer or hold something over her.

She swatted the thought away, realizing she had let what Dalton told her change her attitude toward Nicci. Just as she had let what Nicci said about Dalton influence her feelings about him. This had to stop.

"Don't worry, I wouldn't say anything about what you told me," Nicci said, as if sensing her uneasiness. "We're *friends*. You can tell me anything."

Georgia groaned inwardly, afraid of what was coming.

"I saw the bouquet of flowers in your apartment earlier. Pretty." Nicci was right behind her as they neared the top of the stairs. "Dalton brought them to you, didn't he? Roses were always my favorite. You didn't mention that he'd come by, but I saw him this morning from my apartment window."

"I didn't want to upset you," Georgia said, feeling the hair rise on the back of her neck. Nicci was only a breath behind her.

"You like him."

An icy cold ran up her spine.

"It's all right. You don't have to deny it," Nicci said quickly. "That's why you didn't want to tell me what he told you about me. You want to believe him."

"Nicci—" She'd reached the top of the stairs and now turned, feeling better facing the woman than having her behind her. "I just don't want to be put in the middle of this again. This has nothing to do with me."

Nicci's face seemed to crumble. Tears welled in her eyes. She bit her lip as if to hold them back. The effort was lost. "I saw his pickup on the street tonight. I heard him coming after me. It was so dark, I fell. Look." She shoved back the sleeve of her shirt to reveal scraped skin on her elbow, then pulled up the hem of her capri pants to reveal another scrape on one knee.

"I'm so sorry," Georgia said, feeling herself weaken.

Nicci nodded and wiped at her tears. "I'm the one who's sorry for the way I've been acting. I'm scared. I hate this whole divorce thing. I'm terrible at it." She smiled through her tears. "Forgiven?"

"Of course." Georgia accepted Nicci's hug and they walked down the hall to stop in front of their apartment doors. Georgia opened her door, then hesitated, feeling guilty. Nicci had been through so much tonight. She felt as if she was abandoning her.

Nicci seemed to be waiting, too. She looked as if in another minute she would invite Georgia in for a glass of wine and some girl talk.

"Good night." Georgia stepped into her apartment, closing the door behind her, waiting until she heard Nicci do the same before she locked it and let out the breath she'd been holding.

LATE THE NEXT MORNING, Nicci hadn't called. Dalton had known she would make him wait. Hell, she might not call at all. He was already sick of her games. Why had she looked him up after all these years anyway?

His brothers and probably his father thought she wanted his money. Was it possible she'd gone through the fortune her father had left her and was now here to blackmail him?

While waiting for Nicci's call, Dalton went online and ran a search under the name Nicci Angeles and waited as the cursor blinked.

He didn't know why he hadn't thought of this before, except that he'd still been trying to come to grips with the idea of Nicci being alive.

Today he was thinking a little clearer. Thanks to the Internet, he should be able to find out what Nicci had been up to over the past nine years.

The first reference to Nicci Angeles was an announcement of her birth.

A daughter, Nicci Barron Angeles, was born to real estate magnet Nicholas Barron Angeles and wife, socialite and former actress Roslyn Wells Angeles Saturday, their first. Both daughter and mother are said to be doing well. Nicci is now the sole heir-apparent to the vast Angeles fortune.

Over the years there were a variety of other mentions of Nicholas Barron Angeles, his wife and daughter only in passing at exclusive parties covered by the press.

One article about Nicholas and the fortune he had amassed included several photographs of Nicci on the Angeles Estate outside of New York. One on a tennis court. She wore that look he now recognized when she knew the camera was on her.

A second photograph was of Nicci and her mother. Nicci's gaze was wary as she looked at her mother. Roslyn appeared half drunk and belligerent, the tension between mother and daughter apparent even in a blurry black-and-white on newsprint.

He skimmed through the other instances Nicci's name was mentioned and stopped on the article about her mother's suicide.

That would have been right after daddy dearest deserted both mother and daughter. Nicci would have been seventeen. A year later, her father would be killed in an automobile crash in the Hamptons. The only passenger in the car, a woman slightly older than Nicci and believed to be the rich man's lover, had survived the crash.

News of Nicci's inheritance of her father's fortune was almost lost in the scandal that followed. Dalton realized that he'd met Nicci not long after she'd become one of the richest young women in the world. She had no family and no friends, unless you counted Ambrose. He wondered where she'd picked up Ambrose or if she'd somehow inherited him from her father.

For an instant, Dalton felt sorry for the poor little rich girl. His sympathy passed though at the memory of the night on the boat when she'd tried to kill him.

He continued his search but there were no more mentions of Nicci Angeles. It was almost as if she really had died that night at sea.

NICCI WAS her old self the next morning, insisting on helping Georgia unpack the new boxes Jim Benson delivered. It was the last thing Georgia wanted, but she also didn't want to be at odds with her renter.

Fortunately Nicci hadn't mentioned Dalton or what had happened yesterday all morning. Georgia was hoping they were past that.

Jim was clearly taken with Nicci and hung around longer than usual. "You like sailing?" he asked her, sounding shy as he pointed to the silver sailboat necklace around her neck.

"I love sailing. My father taught me. How about you?" Nicci asked.

"I've never tried sailing," Jim admitted. "But I've always wanted to."

Georgia doubted that. If Nicci had been interested in skydiving, Jim Benson would have been ready to jump right then.

"There are some great sailing schools," Nicci was saying.

"The ones in Seattle aren't that far from here. The Puget Sound School of Sailing is excellent. I highly recommend it."

"You know, I just might go out there on my vacation and take a lesson," Jim said with more enthusiasm than Georgia had ever seen in him.

"Good for you," Nicci said.

"Fort Peck Reservoir is only an hour from here," Jim said, warming to the subject. "Has more shoreline than the state of California and gets its fair share of wind."

"You can often pick up a used sailboat for not much money," Nicci said. "It's very enjoyable. Lots of peace and quiet out on the water."

"Sounds like just what I need. Thanks for the advice."

"You should go out with him. He likes you," Nicci said after Jim left. "I could arrange it."

"No, thanks." She didn't want Nicci arranging anything. "I'm too busy to date."

"Then you should get *un*busy," Nicci said. "You know what they say about all work and no play."

"I've always been dull so it wouldn't change a thing," Georgia said as she prepared for her knitting class.

Nicci laughed but was smart enough to drop the subject. "I need to run some errands. Can I get you anything while I'm out?"

"No, but thank you."

Nicci seemed to hesitate as if there was more she wanted to say. "Well, see you later then," she said and headed upstairs to her apartment to change.

Georgia couldn't help the relief she felt when Nicci was gone. She found herself uneasy around her renter now. She kept thinking about Dalton Corbett's warnings concerning Nicci.

She'd tried to brush them aside, telling herself that

spouses often said terrible things about each other in the heat of a divorce. It was Dalton's concern about Georgia's safety that had kept her awake until all hours last night.

DALTON GLANCED up from his chair on the porch to see Lantry heading his way. His brother didn't look happy. Not much new there. Dalton was surprised his brother hadn't hightailed it back to Texas and his lucrative clients.

"Mornin'," Lantry said as he joined him on the cabin porch. "Let me guess, she hasn't called."

Dalton nodded with a rueful smile. "Maybe something came up." They both laughed.

"The divorce papers are drawn up. You really think she'll sign them?"

Dalton shrugged. "Depends on what she's doing here. Hopefully I'll find out once she calls. I'm worried about the woman she's renting from."

"Georgia Michaels," Lantry said. "I saw her yesterday when she paid you a visit."

Dalton glanced over at him. "You ran a check on her?" He shouldn't have been surprised, but he was.

"Just wanted to be sure that there was no connection in the past between her and Nicci."

"Georgia and Nicci in cahoots?" Dalton laughed.

"Wouldn't have surprised me. The Nicci you've described could use a sweet, innocent-looking young woman to front for her."

Dalton shook his head. "Georgia Michaels is a victim in all this. I'm worried as hell about her."

"I think you should be more worried about what Nicci has planned for you," Lantry said, always the lawyer. "What did this Michaels woman bring you?"

"Nicci told her it was divorce papers, but it was a large manila envelope filled with blank paper."

"Why would she—"

"And some photographs."

"Now we're getting somewhere," Lantry said. "So tell me, little brother, exactly what kind of blackmail are we dealing with?"

"See for yourself," Dalton said, retrieving the photographs from where he'd hidden them.

Lantry glanced through them and swore, his gaze jerking up to meet Dalton's. "What the hell?"

The sudden vibration of his phone actually made Dalton flinch. He snatched it from his pocket and checked caller ID. "It's Nicci."

"Be careful what you say. She might be recording it," Lantry warned.

"Sleep in?" Dalton said, skipping hello.

Nicci chuckled. "Don't you wish you'd been in bed with me?"

"Same way I wish I'd get eaten alive by a grizzly."

"You're in a mood this morning," she said. "Don't you ever think of the two of us?"

"Only in my nightmares." He regretted the words at once.

"You have nightmares about us?" She liked that. He could hear it in her tone.

"Just about you."

She laughed. "Maybe it wouldn't be a good idea for us to meet. You sound a little hostile."

"Not at all. I'm looking forward to seeing you again. After all, you're my *wife*."

"You remembered." Her silver bracelets tinkled, making him think of Georgia Michaels and the silver hoop earrings.

"So let's get this over with. Where and when?"

"I'm as excited to see you as you are me."

"You lie so beautifully."

Nicci sighed. "You always were a charmer. I found the perfect place for us to meet. The locals call it Lover's Leap. It's not far from Trails West Ranch. Think you can find it?"

He knew the spot. So like Nicci to choose a cliff to meet on. "I'll be there waiting for you."

GEORGIA GLANCED at her watch. Agnes, who never missed a class, hadn't shown up this morning. Georgia had grown very fond of the petite elderly woman and was now worried. Agnes lived alone in a huge old farmhouse miles from another living soul. What if something had happened to her?

Getting everyone started knitting and glancing at her watch, Georgia decided that she would give Agnes another five minutes and then she was going to have to drive out to her farm and make sure she was all right.

Everyone turned as Agnes stepped into the yarn shop. "Sorry I'm late," Agnes said, looking harried.

"Agnes!" Georgia rushed over to give her a hug.

Just then Nicci came down the stairs into the shop. She stopped, seeming surprised by what was going on.

"Agnes, is everything all right?" Georgia was asking.

"Well, now that you mention it," Agnes said, taking her usual chair and looking in Nicci's direction. "I had some unpleasant business to take care of this morning. More than a dozen of those trash birds got into something left on my porch."

"They make a mess?" Georgia asked, ready to be sympathetic.

"Worse. Whatever they ate killed them."

A gasp rose from the group.

"How strange," Nicci said, standing at the edge of the group.

"You don't know what killed them?" Georgia asked.

"Not yet. I took several of the birds to my veterinarian. You know he's also the Whitehorse assistant coroner. I'm sure he'll get to the bottom of it."

"How awful," Georgia said. "You say it was something left on your porch?"

"A cupcake in a box like the kind you can buy at the local bakery," Agnes said.

"A cupcake?" everyone said in surprise.

"There must have been something in it that was poisonous to birds," Nicci said.

"That's what my vet said. He said it was a good thing I didn't eat it. As if I would! I'm an old woman, but I'm not a fool!" Agnes looked down. "But I did forget my knitting bag in the car," she added with an embarrassed laugh as she got up to go get it.

"Let me help you," Nicci said and opened the door for Agnes. The two stepped outside, Georgia watching from the window as Nicci took the elderly woman's arm.

Sometimes Nicci could be so thoughtful, she thought, feeling guilty for her less-than-flattering earlier thoughts as Nicci leaned toward Agnes and whispered something.

Chapter Seven

Dalton stood on the edge of the cliff looking down at the Missouri River snaking its way through central Montana. He heard the car pull in and park, the door open and close, the crunch of footsteps advance.

He didn't turn. Had Nicci wanted to kill him quickly, now was her chance. One little push. There wasn't a soul around for miles. Lantry was the only one who knew Dalton was meeting Nicci here. It would be Lantry's word against Nicci's. There wasn't a chance in hell Nicci would fry for his death.

"Nice view," Nicci said, joining him on the precipice.

He didn't turn to look at her. Out of the corner of his eye he saw that she wore the large dark sunglasses he'd seen on her that first day. The breeze coming up the steep rock face from the river ruffled her blond hair. He wondered idly if it was a wig and if that mane of dark hair was beneath it.

He could smell her perfume and knew it was no coincidence she wore the brand she had that night on the boat— the last time they were together.

"Thinking about jumping?" she asked in that mocking tone of hers.

"Actually, I was wondering how long it would take you to hit the bottom," Dalton said.

She laughed and turned toward him. "So what's stopping you?"

He stared at the woman who'd done her damnedest to ruin his life and wasn't through yet. Nicci looked smaller than he remembered. He could see how he'd been fooled by her. No one would believe what she was capable of by looking at this slim, startlingly attractive woman.

He even had trouble believing it standing here now. That night on the water seemed only a bad dream. The fact that she was here now proved nothing horrible had happened, didn't it?

"What's wrong, Dalton?" she asked, smiling as she removed her sunglasses. "Lost your courage?"

One look into those green eyes and he instantly quit deluding himself. He'd tried to kill this woman. The fact that it had been self-defense made it all the more horrific.

"No, I just lost my taste for sick, pathetic women. What do you want, Nicci?"

"Is that any way to be, husband dear?"

"Let's not play games. We both remember the last time we were together."

Her smile broadened. "And we have the photos to prove it, don't we?"

"Blackmail, is that what this is about? Fine. Like I said, what do you want?"

She stepped closer to the edge of the cliff and looked down, then back at him, daring him. One step toward her, one little push and she would fall a hundred and fifty feet to the rocks below.

He took a step back, shaking his head.

"Am I bringing back too many memories for you?"

"My lawyer is drawing up divorce papers," he said.

"Your brother Lantry?"

Apparently she'd done her homework on his family. Could Lantry be right? Was Nicci after the Corbett money?

"Why now after nine years, Nicci? By the way, where's your buddy Ambrose?"

Her smile faded, those green eyes turning to ice. "Maybe I'm here because I thought there might be a chance for us."

"Not a chance in hell."

She cocked her head at him. "I've always wondered— why didn't you go to the police?"

"You know why. You set me up so completely no one would have believed me."

She smiled, clearly pleased. "But you could have had me declared legally dead two years ago and you didn't. I thought by now you would have wanted to settle down with some tiring, dull woman who'd bear your children and make big ranch-style meals for you while you raised your sheep or cows or whatever."

He said nothing.

"You want to know what I think?" she asked.

"No."

"I think you never got over me. I ruined you for other women."

"Not in the way you think," he said.

She laughed and reached out as if to touch him.

He stepped back. "I'm through playing games with you, Nicci. Just sign the divorce papers when you get them. Let's end this like human beings."

"I wish it was that easy, Dalton." She brushed past him.

He stood facing the river, not turning as he heard her leave. A wave of relief washed over him as the sound of her car engine died off in the distance.

For nine years in his nightmares, he'd killed Nicci again and again, each slaying more horrible than the last. She'd proved her theory that night on the boat. She'd turned him into a killer.

Today proved nothing to the contrary.

As he walked back to his pickup, he told himself that all he'd done today was put off the inevitable.

GEORGIA HADN'T REALIZED that Nicci had returned until she saw her standing at the front of the shop looking out the window.

"Nicci?"

The woman didn't seem to hear her.

Georgia started toward her, suddenly afraid that something had happened. It was her expression that made Georgia halt just feet from her. A chill skittered up her spine. "Nicci?"

She turned, her expression changing so quickly that Georgia told herself that she'd only imagined the cold hatred she'd seen. What had Nicci been thinking about? Her marriage to Dalton? Georgia couldn't imagine how love could turn to such hatred. But who else could Nicci have been thinking about?

"Can you sit down for a moment?" Nicci asked and moved to the comfortable chairs Georgia used for her classes.

Georgia took a seat. Nicci was smiling but she could see that the woman's eyes were shiny with tears.

"Is everything all right?"

Nicci nodded, turning up the wattage on her smile. "I was just thinking about my *family*."

Georgia hoped her shock didn't show in her expression. Nicci had been thinking about her family?

"You told me all about your family, your Nana Michaels, but I haven't told you about mine," Nicci was saying. "My father was brilliant. He started with nothing and worked hard and became very wealthy. That's all most people know about him. But I knew the loving, generous man. I was his only child. He adored me and spoiled me. We were so close."

"Has he passed?" Georgia asked, thinking she surely had imagined the look of cold hatred earlier, given the way Nicci talked of her father.

"It was the worst day of my life when I lost him. It was as if my life ended." She looked away.

"Were you close to your mother as well?"

"Oh, yes," Nicci said, brightening. "She was one of those mothers who cooked and sewed even though she could have had someone else do all those things. In fact," she said with a laugh, "my father was always telling her to hire someone to take care of the house and me, but she wouldn't hear of it. I used to sit on the kitchen counter and she would let me help even when I made a mess. She didn't care. She just loved being with me."

"Your childhood sounds idyllic," Georgia said. "You were so lucky."

"Lucky? Yes, wasn't I? I'd hoped to have a marriage like my parents'." She glanced down, tears filled her eyes and spilled over her cheeks.

Georgia took her hand and squeezed it. "I'm so sorry."

"I just don't know why things went so badly. We were both just barely eighteen and so in love."

"That's awfully young to know what you want for the rest of your life."

"I suppose so," Nicci said but Georgia could tell that she didn't appreciate her saying it.

"You're older now, maybe…"

Nicci looked over at her hopefully, then shook her head. "Dalton doesn't love me anymore. I know it sounds corny, but I really thought he was my soul mate. Have you ever had a male soul mate?"

Georgia shook her head and laughed nervously. "Not even close."

"That's why female friendships are so important," Nicci said, squeezing her hand. "I can't believe how fortunate I was to meet you. Men come and go, but women friends never betray you. Promise me we'll always be the best of friends."

"Of course," Georgia said, even though it was a ridiculous promise since Nicci would be leaving town soon.

"Let's go do something fun." Nicci got to her feet. "I've been wanting to go to that hot springs north of town. I love to swim."

Georgia glanced at her watch. "I wish I could, but I have Lamaze class with Rory in an hour. I'm her backup coach."

"Oh, that's right, you told me about that. That's all right, we'll probably get to do it before I leave."

Georgia rose, feeling guilty. "Another time."

"Sure. Oh, I almost forgot." Nicci hurried over to the counter and picked up a long white box Georgia hadn't seen sitting there. "I went shopping. There's the cutest little store just a few doors down." She thrust the package at her.

Georgia put her hands up. "No more presents, really."

"I saw this and it was just so perfect for you, I took a chance even though it was on sale and they won't let me exchange it." She waited, holding out the box.

Georgia had no choice but to take it under the circumstances, but felt irritated with Nicci for putting her in this position. She lifted the lid as an excited Nicci watched, waiting for a reaction.

The sweater was pale yellow.

"It's cotton so you can wear it even in the summer," Nicci said. "Do you like it?"

Georgia actually did. "I love it." That was only a slight exaggeration. "It's beautiful."

Nicci plopped back down in a chair, clearly relieved. "I promise, no more surprise packages."

"Thank you." She glanced at her watch. "Oh, I really need to get moving." Miss Thorp would be coming in to watch the shop at any moment.

Taking the box and sweater, she hurried upstairs to shower and change into casual clothes for the Lamaze class.

She was just coming down the stairs to leave when Rory called.

"Hi, I just wanted to let you know that you don't have to come to Lamaze today."

"I was just heading out the door. What's up?"

"You have enough going on with the shop, you can skip one. Go do something fun. You deserve it. I insist. Gotta go. See you in knitting class tomorrow."

"Oh, okay." Georgia hung up, feeling hurt and confused. Rory had sounded funny. Or was it just Georgia's imagination? She'd been so insistent that Georgia not come.

"Something wrong?" Nicci asked as Georgia finished coming down the stairs.

"I guess I don't have Lamaze after all."

"Really? Great. Let's go swimming at Sleeping Buffalo. I heard they have some fun slides. I really could use a distraction."

Miss Thorp came in just then, so Georgia had no excuse not to go, especially after Nicci had bought her the sweater. "Let me grab my swimsuit and a towel."

"This is going to be so much fun," Nicci said.

LANTRY WAS WAITING for Dalton when he returned from meeting with Nicci. Dalton hadn't realized how worried his brother had been until he saw his relief.

"Well?"

"I met with her." Dalton shook his head.

"You didn't accomplish *anything?*"

"I wouldn't say that." He grinned. "I didn't kill her. Believe me that was a huge step. I didn't even try. It really made her angry."

Lantry stared at him. "You're serious, aren't you?"

"Nicci is one sick puppy. I just wish I knew what she was up to. I have to find out why she waited nine years and what she's been hiding from all these years." Dalton told Lantry what he'd discovered online.

"That *is* odd, one of the rich and famous hiding from the limelight," Lantry drawled.

Dalton had been thinking. "You know I saw her on the news. In some small town in Tennessee. Harvey, Tennessee? A cop was leading her through a crowd."

His brother sat up. "You think she was arrested?"

"I don't know. When I saw her, I thought I was just imagining things, but it brought back the nightmares."

Lantry was giving him one of those big-brother looks.

"I'm okay."

"Hell, I'm not sure I'd be okay if I'd been through what you have."

"Maybe that's why she's here. She was afraid I'd seen the news and knew she was alive."

"What would she be afraid you'd do?"

"Go to the cops?"

Lantry shook his head. "You didn't go to the cops nine years ago and you haven't now. She has the photographs. Why would she be worried about what you would do?"

He had a point. "Then what the hell does she want? Look, I can't just sit around here and play games with her. I have to get to the bottom of this."

"I wouldn't suggest antagonizing this woman."

"Believe me, just the fact that I'm still breathing antagonizes Nicci."

"Maybe you'd better tell me what you intend to do."

"Maybe I better not," Dalton said as he picked up his keys and headed for his truck. "Something just doesn't feel right about all this."

GEORGIA FELT like a schoolgirl playing hooky. But she had to admit that she enjoyed the hot springs. She and Nicci had gone down all the slides. Nicci was like a fish when it came to water. It was interesting seeing Nicci in her element. As much as Georgia wanted to keep her distance, she couldn't help but be drawn to her.

What surprised Georgia the most was that she hadn't worried about the shop. It had felt very decadent, but good to play for a couple of hours in the middle of the day.

She relieved Miss Thorp, thanking her and feeling only a little guilty when they returned.

"You sound good," Rory said when Georgia called her. "You must have enjoyed your time off."

"I did. How was Lamaze?"

"Fine."

Georgia was still a little hurt that her friend hadn't wanted her to come. "So Devlin was there?"

"He couldn't make it."

"No? Then I should have been there."

"You do enough for me and always have."

What was this about? "You're my best friend. I'm here for you whenever you need me," Georgia said, concerned by the strange tone of Rory's voice.

"Yeah, well, maybe I've taken advantage of you for too long."

"That's ridiculous. Where would you—" her shop's landline rang "—get such an idea?"

"You'd better answer that. I'm glad you had fun swimming. You should do that more often."

"Wait. I want to know what's going on and don't tell me it's nothing. I'm your best friend." The phone rang again.

"Nicci mentioned how overworked you were and that you never had a minute to yourself and how she wanted to get you away from the shop for a few hours because she was worried about you."

"*That's* why you told me not to come to Lamaze?" Georgia was furious. She couldn't believe Nicci had done that.

The phone rang again. "She's just worried about you and so am I," Rory said. "You *don't* get out of that shop at all. You really need to answer your phone."

"I *love* going to Lamaze with you. There is nothing I would rather do. We will talk about this later." Georgia sighed as she snapped off her cell phone and reached for the landline.

As she picked up the phone, she looked up to see Nicci return from the liquor store with two bottles of wine. "For after the movie," she mouthed.

DALTON CALLED, unwilling to take a chance of running into Nicci by stopping by the yarn shop. As the phone rang, he told himself he wasn't doing the same thing as Nicci—using Georgia.

"In Stitches."

The moment he heard her voice he almost changed his mind. "Don't hang up. It's Dalton Corbett. Are you still there?"

"Yes?"

"I need to talk to you. Is there any chance you can get away? Please. It's important for your sake as well as mine."

"When?"

"Now?"

"I think I can arrange that. Where would you like the yarn delivered?"

Nicci was there. He was amazed Georgia had agreed to meet him. Something must have happened. Or had she simply given what he'd told her some thought? He could only hope.

"Do you know where Nelson Reservoir is?"

"Yes. I can deliver that order myself. Give me twenty minutes."

"Thank you."

"No problem. See you soon."

Dalton hung up, hoping to hell he hadn't put Georgia in a worse position. He would just have to make sure neither of them was followed.

GEORGIA HUNG UP the phone and looked at Nicci still standing in the shop smiling at her. "I just talked to Rory."

"Oh, is that who that was?" Nicci said. "You should have told her hi from me."

"You told her I was overworked."

"You are."

"But I don't consider going to my best friend's Lamaze class work."

"Georgia, when was the last time you did something just for fun, no obligation for a friend, just a couple of hours for yourself? We had fun at the pool, didn't we?"

"I'm not arguing that. I really don't appreciate you changing my plans for me."

"Come on, you had fun today and Rory was fine without you, wasn't she?"

"Yes, but—"

"See? There was no harm done. Rory understood. We both care about you and tonight we're all going to the show together. Don't be angry. Rory and I really thought we were doing you a favor."

Was that all this had been? A thoughtful gesture? Or had Nicci manipulated the situation to get what she wanted— Georgia to go to the hot springs with her?

"I appreciate the thought, but in the future—"

"Don't worry," Nicci said. "I get the message."

Georgia listened to Nicci's irritated footfalls on the stairs, her stomach roiling. Since Nicci had come into her life there'd been way too much drama and Georgia felt as if she were about to make it worse by meeting Dalton Corbett at the lake.

Hurriedly, she put together an order just as she would any customer, all the time questioning her judgment. But in truth, she needed to talk to someone who knew Nicci. Her manipulative behavior scared Georgia. And Dalton's warnings about the woman only made her more apprehensive about her renter across the hall.

"I'm sorry, Agnes, but there isn't anyway to know what killed the birds you brought me," the veterinarian said when she stopped by.

Agnes couldn't hide her disappointment.

"Now, I can send the contents of the bird's stomach to the state lab, but that is going to be expensive and take several weeks and there's a good chance if the bird was poisoned, the poison won't show up," he said. "Now if it had been a dog, there would be obvious signs, but a bird…"

Two weeks was too long to wait. "So there's nothing else I can do?"

"If you think someone is poisoning your birds, then you ought to let the sheriff know."

Agnes recalled the harshly hissed words Nicci had whispered into her ear only that morning in front of the knitting shop, when she'd walked her out to her car to get her knitting bag.

Who's going to believe a demented old woman without proof? You have any proof, Agnes?

"Thank you, John," Agnes told the vet. "I guess the birds just got into something that didn't agree with them."

"More than likely, Agnes. More than likely."

Chapter Eight

As Georgia drove north out of Whitehorse, the lush green wheat and grasses bowing to the breeze, she kept an eye on her rearview mirror. No sign of Nicci's rental car. There was little traffic on the two-lane road, but still Georgia felt nervous.

The rolling prairie ran north toward the Larb Hills, a postcard panorama under the blue of the big sky. She put down her window and let the warm summer-scented air blow in, feeling a strange excitement mixed with fear about going to this clandestine meeting with Dalton Corbett.

They were taking a chance meeting like this. He was a married man in the middle of an ugly divorce. Even if he and Nicci had only been together a week during the entire nine-year marriage and both seemed anxious to divorce, they must have been in love to get married.

She was walking a very thin line, still determined not to get involved in their marital problems, but at the same time, she needed to know more about her renter. Dalton had scared her yesterday—just not as badly as Nicci had last night. And this issue with the Lamaze class had left Georgia shaken.

Dalton didn't need to convince her that Nicci liked to get her own way. Or that she acted badly if she didn't.

Nicci had lied to her about not being able to get on the ranch. Now Georgia wondered what else Nicci had lied about, including seeing Dalton's pickup after the movie and running from him.

Nelson Reservoir was north of town. Dalton hadn't said exactly where to meet him, but she figured it would be near the campground and boat ramp.

She used to come out here with Rory and her parents when they were kids. Then Rory's little sister had disappeared. Kidnapping was unheard of in Whitehorse, but the little girl was never found. Not too many years after that, Rory lost both of her parents in an automobile accident.

Georgia had never known her own mother or father. She'd been left on Nana Michaels's doorstep when she was but a few hours old. No one had ever stepped forward to claim her. She had always suspected her mother had to be someone from Whitehorse because she'd left her on a kindly widow's doorstep. How else could her mother have known that she would be lovingly cared for?

There were a couple of trailers in the campground, one tent, and several pickups and boat trailers in the parking lot at the boat ramp.

The lake lay like a crystalline blue puzzle piece, a perfect fit in the prairie basin. Trees lined the shores, a few cabins among them on either side of the campground.

A boat motor could be heard putting along on the opposite shore. Another boat could be seen just to the south of a small island she'd always called Bird Island because of all the gulls and pelicans that congregated there.

Other than the boat motor, there was no sound this afternoon and no one around—including Dalton Corbett.

Georgia parked facing the road in and cut her engine.

She'd left while Nicci was in her apartment, taking the bogus order with her in case Nicci was watching from upstairs.

Georgia wished she hadn't agreed to go to the movies.

"I know I'm not going to be in town long, but I'd still like to get to know Rory better," Nicci had said, catching Georgia at a weak moment.

Georgia had just seen how kind Nicci had been to help Agnes get her knitting bag out of the car. Clearly Agnes had been shaken after her horrible experience with the dead birds.

"I'll ask Rory about the movie," Georgia had said.

"Great. Last time I was in a funk. I'm really looking forward to this. Call Rory now. Please?"

Georgia had and Rory had agreed to come in from her horse ranch for the movie.

Nicci had been beaming and it had seemed like such a small thing to agree to. But then Nicci had canceled her Lamaze class with Rory and now Georgia felt troubled about the woman again.

She glanced at her watch, getting more anxious by the minute. If Nicci found out about this meeting with Dalton, she'd see it as a betrayal and there would be even more trouble. Georgia didn't need more trouble from her renter. This *was* a bad idea. Maybe she should—

Dust rose along the road into the campground. A pickup approached. Georgia was relieved to see Dalton behind the wheel and at the same time nervous.

He parked next to her and got out. "I thought we could take a walk."

"Okay," she said, glad he hadn't suggested talking in one of their rigs.

They walked down the dirt road through the trees and campsites, grass growing up between the ruts. A breeze ruffled the surface of the water, scenting the air.

"Thank you for meeting me," Dalton said after a few steps. "I hated to put you on the spot the way I did."

He slowed, glancing over at her. He couldn't have looked more handsome, his Stetson shoved back to expose the tanned sculpted lines of his face and those amazing blue eyes.

"I'm going to put you on the spot some more and I apologize for that, but I have to know what Nicci is doing in Whitehorse and I thought maybe you—"

Georgia stared at him in confusion. "The *divorce*."

He was shaking his head. "The envelope you brought me was full of blank sheets of paper. Nicci just wanted you to believe that's what was inside it."

"That's not possible." But even as she said it, Georgia knew that it was. "Why would she—"

"Look, I'm not trying to put you in the middle of this again, but I need to find out what she wants from me. Did she mention where she's been the last nine years?"

Georgia was still dumbfounded over what he'd told her about the contents of the envelope. She believed Dalton. He'd been honest with her about the cut tires while Nicci had lied about not being able to get into Trails West Ranch. And now Nicci had lied again.

"I got the impression she'd been out of the country."

He nodded and sighed. "Who knows if that's true? I checked the Internet. It's as if she really *did* die nine years ago. What about her rent? Was the check from a bank in the states?"

"She paid in cash."

He chuckled. "I should have known. Did she fill out a rental application or show you her driver's license?"

Georgia shook her head. "Sorry."

"You didn't get references?"

"No, I—"

"It's okay. I know how Nicci can be." His smile was warm and reassuring.

"You must think I'm incredibly naive," Georgia said.

"Not at all."

"Well, *I* think I am," she said with a laugh. "My friend Rory pointed out to me that I know nothing about the woman who is living just across the hall from me in my own building. I thought I knew her, but now…"

"She's done something to scare you."

She frowned at him. "Why would you say that?"

"What did she do?"

Georgia turned to look out at the lake. "I feel as if I'm betraying her trust by talking to you about this."

"I'm worried about you or I wouldn't ask. But if you don't want to tell me…"

"It's just that after I took the papers out to you, she wanted to know everything you said to me."

"You didn't tell her."

"No. How did you know that?"

"She finally called me. We met and I could tell she was angry that she didn't know what I said to you. I told her I didn't say anything, that this has nothing to do with you."

"Thank you." They reached the end of the road and stopped again. Nearby ducks splashed in the shaded shallows and farther out, a gull cried as it skimmed over the water's surface.

"But it does have something to do with you. It did from the minute she ducked into your store and got you to cover for her. I'm sorry," he said quickly. "I wasn't criticizing you. Just stating a fact."

"I really don't understand what's going on."

"That makes two of us." He sighed as they started the walk along the lake back toward their vehicles.

"I have to ask you, were you in town last night?"

Dalton looked surprised. "No, why?"

"Nicci said she saw your pickup parked down the street and that you chased her down the alley to the shop." Georgia saw by his expression that Nicci had lied again. "She got skinned up after falling down in the alley trying to get away from you, she said."

He shook his head, his gaze as soft as a caress. "She's trying to get your sympathy. She must feel you pulling away."

"She would go to that kind of extreme? Hurting herself?" But even as Georgia said it, she knew Nicci would. And had.

"I wish I could explain Nicci. I just know that she seems to latch on to a person and doesn't let go. The harder you try to get away, the more insistent she becomes to the point of an obsession."

"Is that what she did with you?" Georgia asked.

"Yeah." His gaze met hers and held it for a long moment. "You sure you want to hear this?"

"No, but maybe I need to."

He stopped as a flock of white pelicans flew over blotting out the sun for a moment. "I met Nicci in Galveston in a sailing bar. I guess I don't have to tell you how she takes over your life the minute you meet her. At first, you like her."

"She has a way of making you feel special and close to her, as if you've known her your whole life."

He nodded and smiled. "Exactly. But then things start to sour if you don't go along with the program or if you listen to anyone who might talk some sense to you about her."

Georgia felt her stomach tighten at his words. She thought of Rory and her feeling that Nicci was trying to put a wedge between them.

Dalton was studying her. "You know what I'm talking

about, don't you? Nicci demands complete control over you. Cross her and…well, let's just say you'll regret it."

"You make her sound dangerous."

"She *is* dangerous," Dalton said. "I woke up married to her, wondering how it had happened. I didn't find the drug she'd given me until two days later on our honeymoon at sea when I got suspicious and switched wine glasses with her."

"She *drugged* you?"

He met Georgia's gaze. "Nicci does whatever it takes to get what she wants."

"She must have been desperate, afraid of losing you. If she loved you that much—"

Dalton laughed. "It wasn't about love. It was about losing. Her father walked out on her and her mother. Her mother killed herself."

Georgia gasped. "She told me about how close she was to her parents."

He was shaking his head. "She seldom saw her father and her mother, well, Roslyn was an alcoholic. Her mother committed suicide not long before her father was killed in a car wreck with his girlfriend. Nicci was raised by a string of nannies. I suppose that's why she can't stand to let go of people. She's desperate to hold on to someone in her life, even if it's a strangle hold. It's when you realize your mistake in getting that close to her and try to pull away that the real Nicci comes out. A psychiatrist would have a field day if he could get Nicci on his couch."

"How awful," Georgia said, feeling worse than before. She'd hoped talking to Dalton would relieve her mind. Apparently this wasn't about anything as simple as signing divorce papers. "You realize you're scaring me."

"Sorry, but you need to know what you're up against,"

he said as they started back toward their vehicles. "Nicci will be served divorce papers in the next day or so. If that's what she came here for, then all she has to do is sign them and leave town."

"You don't believe that's going to happen."

"No, I wish it were. If I knew her real reason for being here—and where she's been…"

"I'm sorry I haven't been more help."

They had reached the pickups.

"Hopefully, she will be out of your hair soon," Dalton said. "I feel responsible for this. If I had stayed in Texas—"

"I befriended Nicci. You had nothing to do with that. I can ride this out if you can."

He smiled at her. "I like your spirit." His smile faded. "In the meantime, I would suggest you play it cool. If you try to pull away from her, it will only make it worse."

"I'm going to the movie with her and another friend tonight. I thought it best if I didn't try to get out of it."

"I think that's smart." He sighed and looked hesitant. "I need to warn you about something else. Nicci has a friend. She calls him Ambrose. If you see her with a man you don't recognize as a local or hear her on the phone with him, I'd appreciate if you let me know. I'm pretty sure she wouldn't have come here without him."

"This man is also dangerous?"

Dalton nodded. "And I wouldn't mention our meeting to Nicci."

Georgia laughed. "Not a chance."

"Oh, one more thing," he said looking sheepish. "I wanted to make sure neither of us was followed. I disabled her rental car. She's probably going to be upset. But if you are horrified by my behavior, it might help between you and Nicci."

Georgia couldn't believe this. "Nicci's going to be furious with you."

"I couldn't take the chance she might follow you," Dalton said. "I already know how she feels about me. I didn't want to take any chances with you."

Georgia felt her face heat. "Thank you, I guess."

He chuckled. "Just watch yourself around her. I'm trying to get this resolved as quickly as possible for your sake."

"I appreciate that, but I'm fine."

His look said he wasn't so sure about that. "I want you to stay that way." His gaze warmed her to her toes. "Look, if for any reason, day or night, you need help, call me. I put my cell phone number on the card with the roses I gave you. Do you still have it?"

"I never saw any card. It must have fallen out when I took the roses upstairs." Her eyes widened with the realization of who had found it.

Dalton shook his head. "Of course, that's how Nicci got my cell phone number to call me. She must have found the card and taken it." He pulled out a business card and handed it to her.

She took the card hoping she wouldn't need help. She felt a little better as she climbed behind the wheel and headed back toward Whitehorse. At least she didn't feel as if she was in this alone anymore. All she could hope was that once Nicci received the divorce papers she would leave town.

A woman like Nicci would want to move on, wouldn't she? But then again, Georgia didn't know what had really brought her here to begin with. That worried her as she drove back to town.

She wished she hadn't agreed to go to the movie tonight because she'd involved Rory. But Dalton had said to play it cool and it was just a movie. She planned to keep busy in the meantime and be busy from now on until Nicci left.

As she pulled into her parking space behind the yarn shop and cut off the engine, she reached for her cell phone to call Rory and tell her the news.

The tap on her side window made her start, but nothing like what it did when she saw who was standing next to her truck.

Nicci smiled and motioned for her to lower her window.

Since she already had the keys out of the ignition, Georgia opened her door, forcing Nicci to step back to let her exit.

"Hi, Miss Thorp said you'd gone out on a delivery. Not one of your students from class?"

"No. An elderly woman I know." She realized the bag with the yarn in it was still on the seat—and Nicci had seen it. "She decided she'd like to come in next week and pick out something else," Georgia said, improvising.

"That was rude of her."

"Oh, I don't mind. She's a good customer." Georgia couldn't tell if Nicci believed her. It angered her that she was forced to lie to her renter about where she'd been and what she'd done.

Soon, it would be over, she told herself. Nicci wouldn't want to stay in this small western town much longer. Already she seemed restless.

"We should go to dinner before the show, some place fun, my treat," Nicci said.

"I'm sorry, I can't."

"Oh?"

Georgia came up with the first thing that crossed her mind, determined to spend as little time as possible with Nicci. "I'm having dinner at a friend's."

"Rory's?"

Georgia was caught in one lie, she didn't want to make it worse by involving another friend. This was getting ridiculous. She hated lying and she was tired of having to explain herself to Nicci. Nor was she going to feel guilty for not including Nicci. Especially when Rory had never even invited *Georgia*.

"Yes, Rory." Georgia picked up the bag from the seat and headed toward the shop. Once inside, she struck up a conversation with Miss Thorp. If Nicci followed her inside, Georgia didn't see her go up the stairs.

Then she remembered. Dalton had disabled Nicci's car. Georgia braced herself. All hell was about to break loose.

"I JUST HEARD from the chief of police in Harvey, Tennessee," Lantry said when Dalton returned to the ranch after seeing Georgia. "He faxed me Nicci's mug shot. She was going by the name Nicci Sherwood."

"That was her mother's maiden name," Dalton said and took the sheet of paper his brother handed him.

"Is that her?"

"Oh, yeah."

"She was arrested for speeding, resisting arrest and trying to bribe an officer in Tennessee two weeks ago. It probably made the news because it was a small-town scandal."

"Was she alone?" Dalton asked and held his breath for the answer.

"Funny you should ask. Her traveling companion was a Taylor K. Ambrose."

Ambrose. So only two weeks ago Nicci had been with him.

"Nicci skated on the charges after bringing in a high-priced lawyer and paying a load of fines."

"Any way to get a description of this Ambrose?" Dalton asked.

"The chief didn't have any more information than that since the passenger was released at the scene. The arresting officer is on vacation, not expected back until the end of the week. I'll see if I can reach him. In the meantime…"

"Yeah, I'll cool my heels."

"Want to tell me where you went earlier?"

"I met with Georgia Michaels. She didn't know much about her renter. Nicci's starting to scare her."

"We'll get the divorce and you'll be free of her. So will Georgia Michaels."

Dalton nodded, but he feared just as Nicci had said when they'd met that it wouldn't be that easy—especially since he now had a pretty good idea that Nicci was still traveling with her sidekick, Ambrose.

If she'd been with him just two weeks ago, then what were the chances Ambrose wasn't close by, waiting?

Waiting for what, though?

GEORGIA HAD CALLED ahead to let Rory know about the myriad lies she'd been telling—including the one about dinner.

Now as she pulled up to Rory and Devlin's ranch house, she could tell Rory had been waiting impatiently for her.

Before Georgia could get out of her pickup, Rory came out to meet her with a look Georgia knew only too well. Rory looked way too pleased with herself.

"What? Did you actually cook dinner yourself or something?" Georgia asked her best friend. Rory was notorious for her lack of interest in cooking. "You shouldn't have cooked."

"Don't worry, I didn't," Rory said with a laugh. "We'll

go to a fast-food place before the movie. Anyway, I have something much better than food."

"Something better than food?" While Rory didn't cook, she *did* love to eat. "This must be good."

"You are not going to believe what I found out."

Georgia laughed. Rory, who was very pregnant, looked as if she was bursting at the seams in more ways than one.

"You mentioned that Nicci told Jim Benson about a sailing school in Seattle?" Rory said excitedly. "Well, I called it to see if they'd ever heard of Nicci."

"I'm not sure that was a good idea." Georgia had warned Rory earlier that Dalton felt Nicci was dangerous. It was just like Rory not to take that seriously.

"What did you say to the people at the school?" Georgia asked, worried.

"Just that I was interested in classes when I come out to Seattle. I asked a lot of questions. The classes are really expensive, definitely only for the wealthy. Then on a hunch, I said, 'I know someone who spent some time at your sailing school.' I described her and said, 'Her name was Nicci, spelled *N-I-C-C-I*. Oh, what was her last name?' 'Corbett?' asked the woman. Bingo!"

Georgia grabbed her friend's arm in surprise.

Rory nodded and grinned. "She *taught* sailing there under the name Nicci Corbett *nine* years ago."

Georgia let go of Rory, stunned. "She hid in plain sight. Still, she's rich, or at least she was according to Dalton, so why would she go to work at a sailing school?"

Rory was like a little kid on Christmas morning, practically jumping up and down. "What better way to meet your *next* husband?"

"No."

"*Yes.* I came up with a story about how Nicci and I had

become really close friends while I was taking lessons at another sailing school where she taught and that I would love to get in touch with her."

"Rory," Georgia said, getting scared for her friend. "What if Nicci finds out?"

"Don't worry, I used a fake name. Anyway," Rory said, ushering Georgia onto the ranch house porch, "the woman told me that Nicci had gotten married. His name was Michael Farmington, a wealthy real estate investor ten years Nicci's senior."

"She's a *bigamist!*"

Rory was shaking her head. "Not technically. At least not anymore. The husband died in a boating accident on their honeymoon. What if she killed him?"

"Rory—"

"She could be a black widow."

Georgia was shaking her head. "Nice theory, but clearly she doesn't kill *all* her husbands."

"Maybe Dalton Corbett was the exception."

Chapter Nine

Dalton hadn't expected to hear from Georgia so soon.

"I have to talk to you. It's about Nicci," she said. "I've found out something. I'd rather not get into it over the phone."

"Of course." She sounded strange. "You're all right, though?"

"Yes, it's just some information that my friend Rory discovered that I thought you should have right away."

"Tell me where to meet—"

"I'm almost to your ranch."

"Great. See you soon then." He hung up filled with a mixture of dread and excitement at the thought of seeing Georgia Michaels again.

"Dalton," Lantry called from the cabin next door. "You going up to supper? Come on, I could use a drink."

"Georgia is coming out."

Lantry raised a brow.

"It's about Nicci."

He groaned. "You want me to wait?"

"No," Dalton told him. "Tell the family I might be late, but not to wait on me."

"Bring her up. I'll tell Juanita to set another plate,"

Lantry suggested. "Whatever she wants to talk to you about, it can wait until after supper. Juanita made sour-cream chicken enchiladas and pork-chile verde with home-made refried beans and Spanish rice."

Dalton laughed. All of the Corbett brothers loved Juanita's cooking. Their father joked that it was her cooking that had got them to Montana—and enticed them to stay—instead of anything to do with him and family.

Turning at the sound of Georgia's pickup, Dalton couldn't help being worried. She had sounded strange on the phone. Whatever she'd come out to tell him was bad news, he could count on that. Otherwise, Georgia would have told him on the phone.

But at least he knew she was safe—as long as he could keep her here on the ranch.

His stomach growled. "Okay, I'll ask her to supper. Warn the family."

THE LAST THING Georgia expected was to be invited to supper. She'd tried to decline, but Dalton wasn't having any of it.

"Whatever you've come to tell me is going to spoil my appetite, sure as hell," Dalton said. "So do me this one favor, have supper with me and my family, then we can talk."

"Thank you, but—"

"I'm starved and Juanita cooked my favorite meal," he'd said, a twinkle in his eye as he gave her a rundown of the menu. "Tell me you like Mexican food. *Please.*"

"I've never had anything more than a taco at a fast-food restaurant and I suspect that's not what you're talking about," she said, embarrassed.

"What?"

"I'm a Montana girl. I've lived in Whitehorse, Montana, all my life except for a few years in college in Havre and if you haven't noticed we're a little short on Mexican food restaurants."

"The closest one I'm told is two hours away."

She laughed. "So there you go."

"Okay, then you are in for a treat. No one makes Mexican dishes like Juanita." He took her arm and steered her toward the main house.

"What will your family say with me dropping by right at suppertime?"

"You're about to find out," he said, grinning over at her as he opened the front door.

Georgia was hit with the most delectable smells. As she breathed in the wonderful aromas, she heard voices. "Dalton, your family will think I have no manners."

He laughed as they came around a corner and into a large living room that looked out over the ranch. "My family will be delighted." Georgia had never been in the main house at Trails West Ranch. It was wonderfully Western from the patina wood floors to the rock fireplace and original log walls.

The room was full of people. Georgia stopped short, but Dalton took her hand and drew her in.

"Everyone, this is Georgia. I invited her to supper."

"That's wonderful," said a blond, blue-eyed, fifty-something woman Georgia took for Dalton's stepmother. "I'm Kate," she said warmly, taking Georgia's hand. "We're delighted you could join us."

"Told you so," Dalton whispered next to Georgia's ear.

"Juanita made Dalton's favorites tonight," Kate said. "But I'm sure he told you that."

"He did," Georgia said, feeling some of her shyness evaporate as she was introduced to each member of the Corbett clan. Dalton's father Grayson, a handsome gray-haired man welcomed her as warmly as the rest of the family and so did Dalton's brothers.

Georgia knew from her friends Maddie and Faith that all the Corbett brothers were gorgeous. Shane, a local sheriff's deputy, was engaged to Maddie Cavanaugh; Jud, the former stuntman, to Faith McKenna. Lantry Corbett was the lawyer and Russell the rancher.

"Georgia owns the yarn shop in town," Dalton said after she'd been introduced to everyone. "She teaches knitting and crocheting and embroidery as well."

She had to smile that he remembered what she'd told him the second time they'd crossed paths.

"Tell me about your knitting classes," Kate said excitedly. "I've always wanted to learn."

Georgia did, surprised by how comfortable she felt after being so embarrassed about arriving at suppertime. The Corbetts had that effect on people, she thought as she looked around the room, her gaze coming to rest on Dalton.

He seemed like a different man here with his family. Happy. Content. Nicci could have had all this, Georgia thought. Or maybe she couldn't have. Maybe Nicci had never found any place that she could be content, let alone happy.

"Well?" Dalton said after dinner when they were walking back to his cabin. "What do you think of Mexican food? Be honest. I can take it."

"I loved it. All those flavors. It sure beats meat and potatoes."

He laughed, a wonderful sound in the cool summer night. Somewhere close by crickets chirped in the tall green grass. The evening sky swept from horizon to horizon with a vastness that made everything about this moment seem extraordinary.

"My family *loved* you," Dalton said quietly. "I wouldn't

be surprised if Kate didn't show up at your next knitting class."

"You are so lucky, having such a big family."

"You don't?" he asked.

She could feel his gaze on her. She shook her head. "I was raised by Doreen Michaels. She was a widow here in town. She died seven years ago. I was left on her doorstep when I was only a few days old. She was a kindly widow who took me in and looked after me. She was the one who taught me to knit."

"She did more than that," Dalton said. "She raised you into a fine young woman. She must have been very proud."

Georgia looked over at him, surprised at his reaction to her story. His gaze touched her face like a caress. She couldn't speak for a moment, her throat choked with emotion. "Thank you. I had a nice time this evening." She'd enjoyed herself so much that she'd almost forgotten why she'd come out here.

Dalton must have been thinking the same thing. "I hate to spoil this evening by talking about anything or anyone unpleasant, but you wouldn't have come out unless it was important."

She nodded. "It is. It might give you the leverage you need with Nicci. You said you couldn't find anything on the Internet? That might be because she was using the name Nicci Corbett."

He let out a curse. "She was using *my* name? I never dreamed she'd do that after what had happened."

"Only until she remarried." Georgia told him how Rory had called the sailing school in Seattle.

"Remarried?" Dalton was shaking his head. "But we are still married."

"That's why I thought maybe you could use the information as leverage to force her to go through with the divorce," Georgia said. "Not that this is any of my business."

He smiled and stepped to her, taking her shoulders in his big hands. "Nicci and I made it your business. I'm sorry. But thank you. I definitely can use this information."

"Good," she said, too aware of the warmth of his hands on her shoulders.

"So this Farmington she married. Where is he?"

"Her husband was lost at sea in a sailing accident on their honeymoon. His body was never found."

Dalton looked as if he'd been slammed in the chest by a wrecking ball. He let go of her and stepped back, turning to grab the porch railing as he leaned over it as if he thought he was going to be sick.

"Dalton? Are you all right?" Georgia asked touching his back.

When he turned, he seemed to have composed himself. "I'm sorry. I'm okay."

He wasn't, though. She could see that and realized he must be remembering his own honeymoon night with Nicci at sea and the reason he thought Nicci had been dead the last nine years.

Dalton tried to pull himself together. A husband lost at sea. That could have been him. He needed to be alone and yet just the thought of sending Georgia back to that shop where Nicci—

He glanced at his watch and frowned. "Are you still planning to go to the movies with Nicci?"

"With Nicci and Rory," Georgia said with a groan. "I completely forgot about the movie. If I hurry…" She looked up at him. "I don't want to leave you like this. I can tell you're upset."

"I'll be fine." He had been about to tell her to cancel.

He'd forgotten her friend Rory would be there. It was better that she go. If she started behaving oddly it would put Nicci on alert and Dalton was afraid what she might do.

And yet, he needed to be completely honest with Georgia, tell her everything, even though he hadn't even told his lawyer everything. "Are you going to the county fair tomorrow?" he asked.

"I have a knitting class in the morning, but then I'm closing up the shop and going." A lot of businesses closed in Whitehorse since the entire county would be at the fair the next few days.

"Look me up when you get to the fair. I'll be in one of the barns."

"All right." She still was studying him with concern.

He tried to put on his best face. "I'm so glad you joined my family for supper. It's one of the most pleasant evenings I've had in years," he said as he walked her to her pickup.

"Thank you. You've made a Mexican food convert of me."

"Georgia, I know it's going to be hard, but you need to act as if nothing has changed with Nicci. I'll make sure the divorce papers are served tomorrow with the new information. With luck, that will be the end of it and we'll never see Nicci again."

He was praying that would be the case for both their sakes. She started to get into her truck but he touched her arm, drawing her back.

"I wish we'd met under other circumstances," he said. "I'll see you tomorrow. In the meantime, be careful."

GEORGIA CALLED Rory as she left the ranch. "Are you on your way to the theater?"

"Yes."

"We'll have to meet there. Don't forget. We had supper together."

"What did *we* eat?" Rory joked.

"Mexican food with the Corbetts."

"Get out of here. So you met them all? I heard the five brothers are all drop-dead good-looking."

"They are, but no more handsome than that husband of yours."

"That goes without saying," Rory said with a laugh. "So what did Dalton say when you told him what we'd found?"

"Not much. He seemed pretty shaken. We're going to talk tomorrow."

Rory's silence spoke volumes.

"What?" Georgia demanded, although she could guess.

"Whose idea was it to see each other again?"

"He's a *married* man."

"Come on, one week when he was eighteen? You're attracted to him."

Georgia felt a chill, remembering Nicci accusing her of the same thing. "I have to go. See you at the theater. Don't forget about supper."

"What did I cook again?" Rory asked before Georgia could hang up.

"Sour-cream chicken enchiladas and pork-chile verde with homemade tortillas and refried beans, also homemade, and flan for dessert."

"Wow, wasn't I something? I assume everything was wonderful?"

"It was. You didn't have any. They wouldn't agree with the baby," Georgia joked. "You had…"

"Mac and cheese. It's really all Devlin knows how to make."

"Remember, we can't act any differently around Nicci."

"This is so Nancy Drew. I love it!"

Georgia pulled up to the theater just seconds before Rory. Nicci was already standing on the curb waiting.

For a moment, Georgia was worried she'd be upset about them making her wait. Or jealous about the supper she thought Rory and Georgia had shared.

But when Nicci saw them, she smiled and seemed to be her old self, making Georgia relax somewhat. As the evening progressed, Nicci appeared to be in rare form, sitting next to Rory and chatting amiably with her before the movie started.

While Nicci's enthusiasm for the three of them having another night out was catching, Georgia couldn't shake the feeling that Nicci was trying too hard. Or was Georgia just being too critical? Did Nicci sense that things had changed?

Georgia knew she could become paranoid without much effort if she wasn't careful. Nicci was just trying to get back into her good graces. That's why she was trying so hard with Rory.

"I need candy," Nicci whispered in the middle of the movie. "Can I get you anything?"

"No, thanks," Georgia whispered back. Rory just shook her head, completely engrossed in the film.

The movie, a thriller, had Georgia sliding down in her seat and gripping the arms of her chair. As the film raced to its dramatic conclusion, Nicci finally joined them again. Georgia barely noticed how long Nicci had been gone until the credits began to roll and she finally let herself breathe.

"I hate movies like that," she said, laughing.

"You love them or you wouldn't put yourself through them," Rory said, laughing with her.

"They say we like to watch scary movies and read scary

books because it's a way to face our fears safely," Nicci commented as they left the theater.

"Well, it is one way to get our hearts racing," Rory said.

"There is so little in every day life that can give us that feeling, that's for sure," Nicci agreed.

Georgia and Nicci parted company with Rory and headed back toward the apartments.

"I had a great time tonight," Nicci said, smiling. "I'm so glad Rory came in for the movie. It really was a perfect night." She yawned. "I'm beat," she said as they reached the back door of the shop and Georgia pulled out her key.

"Me, too," Georgia said, relieved Nicci wasn't going to ask her to stay up and talk about the movie. Hadn't she bought two bottles of wine earlier today?

They climbed the stairs, Nicci humming a song Georgia didn't recognize. She really *did* seem to be in a good mood. Odd, considering Dalton had disabled her car. Maybe she didn't know yet because she hadn't mentioned it.

What, Georgia wondered, had Nicci in such high spirits? She doubted it was the movie—or the company.

As they said their good-nights and went into their perspective apartments, Georgia found herself worried that Nicci's mood had something to do with Dalton—something bad.

THE NEXT MORNING both Agnes and Rory were late for knitting class. Rory was probably feeling the affects of the junk food at the movie last night and Agnes could be running late again.

Still Georgia worried. She checked her watch after getting everyone else started on their projects. Agnes should have been here by now even if she was running late and it was odd that Rory hadn't called to see how things went with Nicci last night.

Telling herself that she would call Rory later, Georgia still couldn't shake the feeling that something was wrong, given that two of her students were missing—the same two who had misgivings about Nicci. Georgia had more than her share of those and was glad Nicci had gone out early this morning and not returned yet.

When the phone at the shop rang, she hurried to it thinking it had to be Rory calling.

"In Stitches," she answered cheerfully, feeling better already as she anticipated her friend's cheerful voice.

"Georgia?" It was Rory's husband Devlin.

"What's wrong? Is it the baby?" she cried. Behind her, she heard everyone in her knitting class seem to hold their breaths.

"Rory's had an accident."

"Oh God, is she all right?"

"She's okay and the baby is okay," he said quickly. "She was on her way in to class and lost control of the pickup."

Georgia covered her face with her hand and tried to breathe. Rory had been on her way to knitting class? "Where is she now?"

"We're still at the emergency room. Hold on, she wants to talk to you."

"Georgia?"

She began to cry at the sound of her friend's voice.

"I'm fine. The baby's fine. But when your class is over I need you to call me, okay? It's really important."

Georgia got control of herself. "Of course." Something in Rory's voice filled her with apprehension. "But you and the baby are all right?"

"Yes. Georgia, make sure Nicci isn't around when you call."

"Nicci?" she asked confused.

"Promise me, Georgia."

"I promise, but I don't—"

"The brake line was cut on my pickup," Rory blurted. "That's why I went off the road. Georgia, remember last night when Nicci disappeared from the movie for so long?"

"You can't really think—" The rest of the words froze in her throat as she heard the creak of the wood floor as someone entered through the back. She turned to find Nicci standing behind her.

"I'm just glad you and the baby are safe," Georgia said, trying to cover.

"She's *there?*"

The terror in her friend's voice was almost Georgia's undoing. "Right. Everyone here was worried about you."

"I'm worried about *you,*" Rory said.

"You just take care of yourself."

Georgia hung up, shaking.

"Is Rory all right?" her class asked in unison, sounding as scared as Georgia felt.

"She was in an accident, but she and the baby are all right," Georgia said, fighting the sick feeling at the pit of her stomach as she wiped at her tears.

"That's terrible," Nicci said, her gaze intent on Georgia's face. "Was that her on the phone?"

"Her husband called." Not an outright lie.

"Oh, I'm sorry, I thought I heard you mention *my* name."

"Rory had asked him to tell you how much fun she had last night." It was the first thing that came to Georgia's mind. The words came out in nervous jerks. She didn't think she had fooled Nicci for a moment.

Nicci's smile never reached her eyes. "That is so like your friend to be thinking of others at a time like this."

"I'M SORRY I'm late again," Agnes said the moment she stepped into the knit shop. "Car trouble." Nicci trouble was more like it.

She stopped short as she saw everyone huddled around Georgia. "What's wrong?" When she saw Nicci at the edge of the small crowd, she braced herself for the worst.

"Agnes, there was an accident," Nicci said. "But Rory and her baby are all right."

The floor beneath her seemed to buckle. Agnes dropped into one of the chairs and an instant later Georgia was beside her.

"An *accident?*" Agnes couldn't help looking in Nicci's direction. A chill shuddered through her and she had to look away.

"I don't have any of the details," Georgia said, squeezing her hand. "I'm just so glad Rory and the baby weren't injured. But I was worried about *you,* Agnes."

"No reason to worry about Agnes," Nicci said from close by. "She's tough as nails. Aren't you, Agnes?"

Agnes looked up into those unusual green eyes and felt herself shudder inside. Nicci wasn't through with any of them and Agnes feared there was nothing she could do about it.

But she had to warn Georgia. She turned to look in her friend's kind face and saw something that gave her a start. Was it possible Georgia knew about Nicci?

She looked scared—and with good reason, Agnes feared. Once Georgia saw through Nicci…

Agnes had to warn her friend. She knew firsthand what Nicci was capable of. Once Nicci realized that Georgia had seen the truth, Georgia would be at the mercy of Nicci's black heart.

Georgia couldn't wait for her class and Nicci to leave

so that she could call Rory back. This time, she had paid special attention to the way Agnes reacted to Nicci. What shocked her wasn't just Agnes's reaction to Nicci, but Nicci's to the elderly widow.

Nicci almost seemed afraid of Agnes and Agnes clearly was repelled by the woman. It made no sense given that just yesterday, Georgia had seen Nicci help Agnes get her knitting bag from her car.

Georgia's head was spinning after what Rory had told her on the phone. It couldn't be true.

"Georgia, can I speak to you in private for a moment?" Nicci asked as the class ended. Everyone was packing up to leave except Agnes. She seemed to be hanging back for some reason.

Nicci was the last person she wanted to talk to right now. "Sure." Georgia wondered what this could be about. Earlier Nicci had looked displeased that she wasn't wearing the silver hoops. Last night, Georgia had put the hoops back in their box and this morning she wore her favorite pearl earrings again that Nana had given her for her sixteenth birthday.

"I have some business to take care of, but I wanted you to tell Rory how happy I am that she's all right," Nicci whispered so the others couldn't hear. "I want to get something for Rory and the baby. Can you tell me how to get out to her place?"

Georgia felt her pulse jump, her heart a hammer inside her chest. "That isn't necessary."

"Rory's my friend, too," Nicci said irritably. "If you can't tell me, I'm sure someone in town…"

"It's not that," Georgia said. "Rory's not at home yet. She's still at the hospital."

"Oh."

She could see Nicci's disappointment.

"Well, I guess I'll try to catch her there," Nicci said.

As she turned to leave, Georgia couldn't wait to get on the phone to Rory and warn her. Just the fact that Nicci had wanted to know how to get to Rory's ranch…

Nicci turned back at the door. "I suppose I should tell someone… I'm meeting Dalton this morning." She touched her skinned elbow. "You know, in case something should happen."

"I'm glad you told me."

Nicci looked disappointed as if she had expected Georgia to try to talk her out of meeting Dalton alone. Georgia felt as if she'd fallen into another one of the woman's traps.

"Are you sure you should meet him alone?"

Nicci shrugged. "Dalton *insisted*. What choice do I have if I want to get this over with?"

"Maybe you should stop by the sheriff's department and let him know where you're going. If you have reason to think Dalton might get violent…"

"Have you forgotten what he did to my tires?" Nicci demanded, sounding disgusted.

"That's why I suggested you talk to the sheriff."

Nicci flipped her hair back from her face in obvious annoyance. "I can't very well go to the sheriff without proof, now can I? Never mind. I didn't mention this to you because I wanted you to come along. I've dealt with Dalton before. Like Agnes, I'm no fool."

Georgia realized that Nicci must not be aware that Agnes was still sitting in the alcove where the knitting classes were held.

"There's a lot you don't know about me," Nicci said, sounding angry. She opened her shoulder bag and tilted it so Georgia could see the contents.

Georgia gasped at the sight of the gun.

Nicci quickly shut her purse and smiled. "I've learned that with Dalton it's best if I can take care of myself." She cocked her head as if amused. "I guess he didn't tell you that he tried to kill me on our honeymoon." She laughed. "I see that he failed to mention that." Nicci lifted the hem of her shirt.

Georgia recoiled at the sight of the scar that ran for a good four inches down Nicci's side.

"This is why he thought I was dead the last nine years." Her eyes glittered. "He did tell you that, didn't he? He left me to die, bleeding in a shark-filled sea. If I hadn't been picked up by a fishing boat…" She dropped her shirt back over the scar, tears welling in her green eyes. "You don't know him as well as you think you do."

This time when Nicci turned, she kept going right out the door, leaving Georgia in shock. Dalton couldn't have done that to her. Nicci had to be lying. Lying and carrying a gun.

Georgia jumped at the touch of a cold hand on her arm. She'd forgotten Agnes was still in the room. As she turned, she saw that the elderly woman's face was sheet-white.

"You have to get her out of your house before she does any more harm," Agnes said in a small, scared voice as she clutched Georgia's arm. "But you can't let her know that you're on to her."

Chapter Ten

Georgia felt goose bumps rise on her skin at the impact of Agnes's words. Before she could say anything, the back door of the shop swung open.

She knew by the expression on Agnes's face who she'd find standing in the doorway even before she turned to see Nicci.

"Everything all right?" Nicci asked into the deathly silence.

"Fine." Georgia's voice cracked.

Nicci's gaze swung to Agnes and a small smile curled her lips. "Didn't mean to interrupt. I left some papers that I need. I don't know where my mind is today."

Agnes's fingers bit into Georgia's arm.

"Oh, there they are," Nicci said, pointing to a manila envelope on the edge of a small display table near the back of the shop. Georgia hadn't seen Nicci put it there earlier. She was thinking of the last time Nicci had eavesdropped on her. That time Nicci said she'd forgotten her purse.

As Nicci stepped over to the table to pick up the envelope, Agnes let go of Georgia's arm and snatching up her knitting bag, took off out the front door.

Nicci glanced in Georgia's direction, her gaze veering off to follow Agnes to her car. When she looked at Georgia again, she smiled, but those green eyes were like ice. "Agnes seemed upset, didn't you think?"

"The birds," she said quickly. "She's still upset over those dead birds."

Nicci lifted a brow. "Still upset over dead trash birds? I probably should have mentioned this before. The other day when I walked Agnes out to get her knitting, she was talking crazy. I hate to say it, but I think the poor dear might be getting dementia."

Agnes was as sharp as anyone Georgia knew, and she was tempted to say as much but bit her tongue. "I'll keep a close eye on her. Just in case you're right."

That didn't seem to please Nicci. "I can tell you are very fond of her. You two seemed very close when I came in."

"She's just a nice elderly woman who likes to knit," Georgia said.

"Hmm." Nicci chuckled. "She's a lot more than that. I just don't want her upsetting you with her crazy stories about cupcakes and dead birds. I can tell you're not yourself."

"I'm just worried about Rory."

"Rory and the baby are fine, you said. Have you talked to her since?"

"No, I've been too busy."

Nicci glanced at the now empty shop. "I guess this is your chance."

Georgia saw that Nicci meant to stick around until she called Rory. "Actually, her husband said she was going to rest. I'll call her later."

"Give her my regards."

Georgia stepped to the counter as Nicci left and leaned against it for support. She was shaking, heart racing. Both the front and back doors of the shop were open to let in the still cool morning air.

She went to the back door, closed and locked it. Nicci had a key, but at least this way Georgia would have a few seconds of warning before the woman appeared. She closed the front door, locked it and put up the Closed sign. She'd been planning on closing anyway and going to the fair.

Picking up the phone, she dialed Rory's number and, with a start, noticed that Nicci's rental car was parked across the street. Georgia felt her pulse quicken. Nicci had gone out the back door even though her car was parked out front?

She'd come back the same way, saying she'd forgotten the envelope. But Georgia had a feeling Nicci had seen her and Agnes from the front of the store and come in the back hoping to catch what Agnes was saying to her.

So where was Nicci *now?*

"GEORGIA?" Rory said on the other end of the line. "What's going on?"

Georgia hadn't even realized that Rory had answered the phone, she'd been so preoccupied with her thoughts. "I'm going to call you right back." She hung up before Rory could question her further.

For a moment, she stared across the street at the rental car. Sun glinted off the windows. Was Nicci sitting behind the wheel watching the shop?

Georgia turned and walked as casually as she could manage to the back of the shop, picked up her purse and hurried upstairs to her apartment. She didn't feel safe until she'd locked her apartment door behind her. Nicci didn't have a key to this door, but she did all the rest.

Pulling out her cell phone, she called Rory.

"What is going?" Rory demanded.

Georgia had moved to the window. She parted the curtains so she could look down on the main street. The rental car was still parked across the street.

"I was just waiting for Nicci to leave," Georgia said. "All this is making me so paranoid. You can't really think she cut your pickup's brake line."

"Can't I? Think about it. She disappeared for a long time last night during the movie," Rory said.

"That doesn't prove she went outside and cut your brake line."

"You know she could have gone out and come back without anyone noticing. Patty was sitting a few rows behind us watching the movie. There wasn't anyone out front because she'd already closed down the concessions."

The street where Rory had parked her pickup was dark. There were no businesses that would have been opened last night during that time. Nicci *could* have left and come back in without anyone noticing.

Georgia watched the street. Still no Nicci. With a chill, she realized that Nicci could have come in the back door by now and made her way up to her apartment.

"Why would she want to hurt you and the baby?" Georgia asked, lowering her voice.

"Are you kidding? Look what happened with my Lamaze class. Without me around, she could get total control over you."

"Excuse me? I do have a mind of my own," Georgia argued, even though she knew she had let Nicci manipulate her. She'd gone along with things because it had been easier than arguing with Nicci, disappointing Nicci, making Nicci angry.

"Come on, this woman is a master manipulator. Anyone could fall under her powers."

"Not you and Agnes."

"Agnes?" Rory sounded scared.

"Agnes just warned me about Nicci."

"Georgia, if Nicci cut my brake lines, then what will she do to Agnes if she thinks she's saying something against her?"

"Nicci told me she thinks Agnes is suffering from dementia."

"That could be Agnes's saving grace. I hope you didn't argue that Agnes was sharp as a tack."

"I didn't." Georgia was scared. She didn't want to believe this. If she did, then that made her renter far worse than even Dalton thought.

"She would have needed something to cut your brake line," Georgia said.

"The toolbox was on the back of the pickup," Rory said. "Devlin checked. A pair of bolt cutters had been used. There was brake fluid on the bolt cutters—and on a pair of old gloves."

Georgia felt like crying. "But what about her clothing? If she'd crawled under your truck—"

"I've had nothing but time to think about this. She was gone long enough that she could have had time to cut the brake line, go to the apartment a block away and change, and come back before the movie ended."

"The first night we went to the movie," Georgia said almost to herself. "Nicci left and didn't come back for a long time."

Rory let out a curse. "You think she made a dry run that night to see if it was possible?"

Georgia shuddered at the thought, remembering how nice Nicci had been to Rory. If they were right, Nicci was a potential cold-blooded murderer. "We have to call the sheriff."

"Georgia, all we have are suspicions. We need proof."

Georgia caught movement on the street below. "Nicci."

"What?"

"Nicci is coming down the street from the coffee shop," Georgia said, relieved she wasn't in her apartment just across the hall.

"I know all this sounds crazy," Rory said. "That's why we have to find the proof. What is she doing now?"

"She's going over to one of the benches along the sidewalk. It looks like she's going to make a call on her cell phone."

FROM THE FRONT WINDOW of her apartment, Georgia watched Nicci take a seat on the park bench.

"She still there?" Rory asked in a hushed whisper from the other end of the line.

"She's calling someone. I hope it isn't me. No, she's talking to someone now. That's funny."

"What?"

"Since Nicci moved in, she hasn't gotten any calls when I was around—or made anyway. Except for that one the other night after the movie. And the one now."

"So who do you think she's talking to?"

"I don't know. Dalton told me she might have a male friend with her that she's keeping under wraps. Could be him. She's really acting animated, laughing and smiling."

"She's talking to a *man*," Rory said positively.

"She just disconnected and is headed for her car. She looks pretty self-satisfied," Georgia reported.

"Now's your chance to search her apartment. If you can find the clothes she wore last night with some brake fluid on them…"

"Rory, what if she catches me? Who knows how long she'll be gone?"

"This might be your only chance before she has an opportunity to get rid of the clothing."

Georgia knew her friend was right. If there was any chance of getting proof...

As Nicci reached the car, she stopped and turned suddenly to look back. Her gaze shot straight to the second apartment window as if she had sensed Georgia watching her.

"Yikes," she cried, quickly stepping away from the window, horrified that Nicci had seen her spying.

"What?"

"She turned and looked right in this direction."

"Did she see you?"

"I don't think so." Georgia carefully peeked out the window, afraid Nicci would be headed across the street to the apartment. "No, she's leaving." Georgia let out a shaky sigh of relief.

"Just do this quickly, Georgia."

Even the idea turned her stomach. But Rory was right. This might be her only opportunity to find out the truth about the woman living across the hall from her.

GEORGIA OPENED her apartment door, listened to make sure there was no sound of anyone on the stairs, and quickly stepped across the hall to unlock the adjacent apartment door.

She hated what she was about to do. But if Rory was right, if Nicci had caused her accident, there might be some evidence in the apartment that would prove she'd cut the brake lines on the pickup.

Or it could prove that all of her concerns about Nicci were unwarranted. Georgia knew that wasn't likely to happen. She just didn't want to believe that Nicci was capable of such a horrible act. But hadn't she drugged Dalton to get him to marry her? And who knew what had happened on their honeymoon?

Hearing no sound other than the pounding of her own pulse, Georgia opened the door and slipped inside.

It was cool and dark in the apartment, the curtains closed. It took a moment for her eyes to adjust to the dim light.

"I'm in," she said into the cell phone.

The apartment was immaculate—just like the other times she'd been inside it visiting Nicci. On the surface, Nicci sure had seemed like the perfect tenant.

Georgia took a step and heard something crunch under her foot. Looking down she saw what appeared to be one half of a cardboard ticket stub like the ones used for a receipt.

"That's funny," she said, bending down to pick up the only thing in the apartment that was out of place. "I just found what looks like a receipt stub from the local dry cleaners on the floor by the door."

"She had something dry cleaned?" Rory cried. "Why didn't we think of that? Of course she would have taken her dirty clothes from cutting the pickup's brake line to the cleaners as quickly as possible. But that means she had to go first thing this morning."

"She did leave early this morning. I didn't see her take any clothing though."

"I don't remember what she wore to the movie, do you?"

Georgia smiled to herself. Rory could have cared less about clothes. Until she met her husband, Devlin, Rory wore oversize Western shirts and jeans and could have easily been mistaken for a cow*boy*.

"Nicci wore a pair of lime-green capri pants and a long-sleeved white shirt." Georgia loved clothes, although her own wardrobe couldn't prove that, given her limited budget. "Might I point out that a long-sleeved white shirt is a ridiculous outfit to wear if you were planning to cut the brake lines on a pickup truck?"

"She could always roll up the sleeves. Wait a minute, I just remembered something. She was wearing a short-sleeved white shirt last night after the show, I'm sure of it."

"I didn't notice," Georgia said. "I would make a terrible detective."

"But you remembered what she was wearing before that. Now all you have to do is see if the long-sleeved white blouse and lime-green capri pants are in the closet—or at the cleaners. If they have brake fluid on them…"

Georgia hurried to the closet, opened it and stared at all the clothes. Georgia's dream closet; and to think this was only a few items from Nicci's summer wardrobe, since she hadn't planned to stay here long.

Her pulse quickened as she spotted the plastic cleaners bag. Nicci hadn't taken the time to remove the clothing inside.

Lifting the bag, Georgia spotted the lime-green pants and white shirt and felt her heart drop like a stone.

"The outfit she wore is here, but it's already been cleaned. She must have had them put a rush on it this morning."

"Check the slip on the top. Mabel always notes if there are any spots on the clothing. Well?"

The words nearly stuck in her throat as she read, "Grease spot on right leg of pants and right sleeve of blouse."

"Bingo! This proves it, Georgia."

Nicci had changed into something so much like what she'd been wearing that Georgia hadn't noticed—not in a dark theater or on the way back to their apartments.

Georgia felt sick. Here was the proof and yet she knew it wasn't enough evidence. The spots had been cleaned.

There would be no way to prove they were brake fluid. Or that it came from Rory's pickup.

She said as much to Rory.

"You're right," Rory said. "Going to the sheriff will only alert her that we're on to her. You'll be safe as long as she thinks you're her friend... Unless you do something to make her turn on you. Like getting caught in her apartment. Get out of there!"

Georgia closed the closet and turned toward the door, anxious to escape. For all she knew Nicci could be returning at any moment.

Her mind raced. What was she going to do with what she'd discovered?

She heard the door downstairs open and footsteps coming up the stairs. Rushing to the apartment door, she quickly opened it and stepped into the hall, locking and closing the door quietly behind her.

Hurriedly she ducked into her own apartment, closed the door quietly and locked it. Standing with her back against it, she finally let herself breathe as she heard Nicci top the stairs and walk the few steps to her apartment door.

There was the sound of the key in the lock. As the door swung open, light flickered under Georgia's feet from across the hall.

Then there was nothing but silence.

"What's going on?" Rory whispered on the other end of the line.

Georgia shushed her as she listened. Nicci hadn't moved. Why would she just be standing in the hall? Had Georgia left something out of place in the apartment?

"Oh, no," Georgia whispered, tiptoeing away from the door. Stepping into the bathroom, she turned on the shower.

"Georgia, is that water running?"

"We messed up," she said into the phone, thinking of all those old detective movies she and Rory loved to watch. "The cleaners stub. It seemed odd that it was lying on the floor by the door when the rest of the apartment was spotless."

She heard her friend let out a gasp. "She stuck it between the door and the jamb so she could tell if anyone had been in the apartment."

Georgia dropped down to sit on the edge of the bathtub. "She knows, Rory. She knows we're on to her."

Chapter Eleven

"You have to get out of there," Rory cried on the other end of the line. "Now!"

Georgia heard Nicci close her apartment door, then open it again. She held her breath, praying she didn't come across the hall. Nicci's door closed and her footsteps retreated down the hall. She waited until she thought she heard the back door close before she went to the window.

"I think she just left," Georgia whispered into the phone. "Her car is parked across the street. I don't see her yet."

"What are you going to do?"

Her mind raced. "I'm not going to leave this apartment until I know she isn't waiting for me downstairs."

"Good thinking."

"Then I'm going to the sheriff and tell him what Nicci did."

"You might want to give that more thought," Rory said. "Unless he has enough evidence to arrest her—"

"He'll question her and scare her enough to keep her from doing anything else," Georgia argued. "At the same time, I'll have him evict her."

"Didn't you say Dalton warned you against doing anything rash?" Rory asked, sounding scared.

Georgia thought of the gun Nicci had shown her. Unless she didn't have a permit for a concealed weapon, then there was no law against her carrying it. "I need to talk to Dalton before I contact the sheriff."

"Good idea."

"There she is," Georgia said from her spot by the window. "She's headed for her car. Wait a minute, she's stopping to talk to someone."

"Who?"

"I don't recognize her. A tall woman with long blond hair, definitely a tourist from the way she's dressed. The woman appears to be asking directions. Nicci's pointing down the street."

"You know Nicci's been here too long if *she's* giving directions," Rory quipped.

"She's getting into her car." Nicci shot a look back at Georgia's apartment window—just as Georgia had anticipated. Georgia was ready, ducking out of sight. "She knows I've been watching her from the window. She looked again."

"You're scaring me."

"Okay, she's driving away."

"Get out of there! Come stay with me until we can figure out what to do."

"I need to talk to Dalton," Georgia said. "I have to go before she comes back. But I'm worried about you."

"Don't be. Devlin isn't letting me out of his sight. Nicci wouldn't be able to get within a mile of the place."

She didn't know where Nicci was off to now and it scared her. "I have to warn you, Nicci asked how to get out to your place." She could almost hear Rory's shudder.

"We have to stop that woman."

"You just take care of yourself and your baby. No more snooping into Nicci's past lives."

Snapping her phone shut, she grabbed her purse and rushed downstairs to the back door.

Her truck was parked just outside. She slid behind the wheel, locking the doors before she put the key in the ignition. A thought struck her, making her freeze. Dalton said he'd disabled Nicci's car yesterday, but it seemed to be working fine. Nicci must have had someone fix it. Was it the man Dalton had warned her about? Ambrose?

Georgia's pulse thrummed in her ears. Why wouldn't Nicci tell her? Because Nicci didn't trust her even before this happened.

She started the car and drove west toward the fairgrounds just outside of town. Summer wheat and prairie grasses had turned the rolling hills to a vibrant summer green. A breeze rolled through the grass like waves. Overhead in the sea of blue, clouds bobbed along, the summer day so at odds with Georgia's emotions.

Normally she loved summer, the warm sunny days, the rich smells, that feeling of being a kid again. She'd had an idyllic childhood growing up in Montana, wading in the creek, climbing trees, building forts.

In the hot quiet afternoons, she would sit with Nana and learn to knit. Later, after she became proficient at it, they would knit and talk, drink frosty glasses of homemade lemonade and eat tiny cucumber sandwiches. Nana thought cucumber sandwiches decadent after reading about them in a magazine and decided it was what real ladies did.

Georgia had never felt afraid in Whitehorse. Not until Nicci moved in across the hall. She slowed at the turnoff for the fairgrounds, having misgivings about not going straight to the sheriff.

But Rory was right. Georgia needed to produce solid evidence to support her suspicions.

Her only hope was Dalton. She'd had the feeling since the beginning that he knew a lot more about Nicci than he'd told her. She needed to know what she was truly up against with the woman. What had happened on Dalton and Nicci's honeymoon to make him think his wife had been dead the past nine years?

She shuddered, remembering Nicci's scar. Dalton couldn't have done that. Nicci was lying. She had to be.

Georgia realized she was putting all her faith in Dalton Corbett. It was more than the fact that he was the one person who knew Nicci better than anyone. She'd felt something with him, a trust, a closeness, a bond. She was depending on him to know what to do. He had to, she thought as she parked and headed for the livestock barns.

But all that aside, she'd felt something else when she was around Dalton, something she hadn't even mentioned to Rory, she thought with a shy grin. Desire. Just the thought of being in Dalton's arms— She told herself she had more important things to think about as her face heated at the thought of Dalton's mouth on her own.

Anyway, Dalton didn't think of her that way, she told herself. Their only connection was Nicci. Once Nicci was gone…

Georgia concentrated on what she had to tell Dalton about Rory and what she'd discovered in Nicci's closet. If it had been anyone but him, she might have feared he wouldn't believe her. It did sound certifiably crazy.

"Did I mention that I believe my tenant is a homicidal maniac who tried to kill my pregnant best friend because my friend is suspicious of her?"

Or was it even crazier than that? Had Nicci tried to get rid of Rory only because she was Georgia's best friend?

Not that it mattered what Nicci's motives had been.

Georgia knew she should be more worried about what Nicci would do next, especially since the woman had a gun.

AGNES SAT down at her kitchen table and picked up her knitting. A light breeze played at the curtains over the sink. She could smell clover in the nearby field and heard a meadowlark singing from the clothesline.

She should be out at the fairgrounds doing her volunteer work. Her needles clicked rhythmically, the movements of her hands not as calming as they usually were. Through the window, she could see the brilliant blue sky. Not a cloud in sight. The weatherman had said it would remain clear and dry over the next few days.

Agnes knew differently. A storm would blow in late tonight.

She still wasn't used to *knowing* things. Things she didn't need—or want—to know. Just this morning after knitting class she'd stopped at the grocery store. Joe in produce touched her arm when he passed her a ripe melon as he always did when she came in and she knew that he was about to get his heart broken by his girlfriend.

Ella, the clerk who gave her change, would get a another grandson before midnight—the sixth boy. Lloyd at the gas station was about to lose his mother to a fast-talking elderly con man and that awful gossip Ruth Napier wouldn't be long with this world.

Agnes knew all of this to be true. Just as she knew Nicci would be paying her a visit.

She frowned, trying to understand this strange phenomenon that only seemed to work when it felt like it. Wasn't like she could pick a winning lottery number or even say who the next president would be.

She'd just touch someone and know way too much

about them and their lives. With Nicci, though, it was different. The feelings Agnes got with her were much stronger—and frightening.

Thinking back, Agnes tried to remember the first time she'd noticed this new talent of hers. That day out in the garden trying to save her tomatoes when the lightning hit and…and when she woke up on the ground she'd had the strangest thought: Georgia's found a renter for her apartment.

How about that? Agnes smiled to herself, feeling better now that she recalled when it had started and possibly why. Not that she was happy about it.

But the way she saw it, she had two choices. She could sit around bemoaning this new *gift* or she could accept it as God's will. How she was supposed to use it was another question she would have to ponder at some length since she apparently had no control over it.

Agnes paused, knitting needles gone still, as she listened. A vehicle. Headed this way. Nicci.

She listened as the car pulled into her yard, tires crunching gravel, the thrum of a car engine as it slowed to an idle, then silence.

Agnes waited. The car door opened and closed. A few moments later the old wood on the porch creaked under the weight of a foot.

Would Nicci knock? Or simply try the door?

The knock was soft, barely audible. The doorknob rattled, hinges groaning as the door swung in.

"Agnes?" Nicci singsonged. *"Ag…nes?"* She dropped her voice. "I know you're home, you meddlin' old woman. Just like last time."

Nicci stopped in the living room. "Agnes?" Her footfalls came down the short hall toward the kitchen.

Agnes felt as if an icy hand had wrapped around her heart as Nicci rounded the corner.

"There you are, you old dear," Nicci said, moving toward the kitchen table where Agnes sat knitting. "Didn't you hear me knock?"

"I heard you," Agnes said, continuing to knit, praying her hands didn't tremble and give her away. "I was ignoring you. Just like last time."

Her first and only encounter with true evil all alone and face-to-face, Agnes could only treat it as she would a mad dog. She wouldn't run. Nor would she show fear. Because to do either, she feared, could be deadly.

She could feel the woman's gaze on her, but pretended to concentrate on her knitting although it wasn't necessary. It had been years since she'd had to look at the needles when she knitted.

Nicci seemed confused that Agnes didn't appear afraid of her. She'd already treated Agnes as if she was deaf earlier in the living room. Now she really must think Agnes was just a doddering old fool who didn't have the sense to be terrified.

"Did you bring me another cupcake?" Agnes asked.

"No," Nicci snapped with obvious irritation as she pulled out a chair and sat down across the table from her. "But if I had you would damn sure eat it this time if I had to shove it down your throat."

Agnes glanced up at her, not surprised by the outburst. Nicci was no longer pretending to be anything other than what she was. As frightening as that was, it was also a relief. If Nicci was disturbed sufficiently maybe she would make a mistake. Or give up. Either way, Agnes knew this would be over soon.

She feared, though, how it would end and who would have to suffer or die before Nicci was through.

With a laugh, Nicci glanced toward the phone on the wall by the back door as if suddenly understanding. "You called the sheriff as I drove in, didn't you?"

"Maybe," Agnes said without looking up from her knitting.

"Too bad he won't get here in time to save you."

GEORGIA FOUND Dalton in the horse barn. The fair wouldn't start for a while. The only people around were volunteers or participants.

She stopped just inside the door, studying him. He hadn't heard her approach because he was talking to one of the horses. She couldn't hear the soft words he spoke, but she could tell by his tone that he was trying to soothe the nervous horse.

She smiled, touched by this tender man. This was not a man who could hurt anyone, let alone try to kill them.

He must have sensed her presence because he turned and, seeing her, smiled clear up into the blue of his eyes. He gave the horse a final pat before joining her.

Georgia felt a little piece of her heart melt.

"You're shaking," he said with concern as he looked into her eyes. "Something's happened."

She nodded and felt tears fill her eyes.

"Let's get a lemonade and find a cool place in the shade where we can talk," he said, putting his arm around her as they left the barn.

"Tell me what's happened," he said, after he'd purchased two cups of lemonade and found them a spot under a cottonwood tree some distance from all the activity. The sun slanted across the open prairie as the day waned.

Georgia blurted out everything, about Rory's accident, the discovery of the cut brake lines, finding the recently cleaned clothing in Nicci's closet and the weapons she carried in her purse.

Dalton listened, saying nothing, but all the color had drained from his face.

"You aren't surprised."

"No, I wasn't sure how much to tell you about Nicci."

"She's done this before?"

"Truthfully, I don't know."

"Dalton, you told me she was dangerous. You didn't tell me she…" Georgia waved a hand through the air.

"That she was capable of murder? I knew that, but I never dreamed…" He shook his head. "I should have told you everything right away. I just didn't think you would believe me."

Georgia thought about the first time he'd told her about Nicci. She'd thought it was a disgruntled spouse talking. That was back when Nicci had seemed so nice and normal. "You're right. I wouldn't have believed you."

He pulled off his Stetson and raked a hand through his hair as he looked toward the fairgrounds. The carnival rides gleamed in the last of the day's sun. Soon lights would begin popping out across the fairgrounds.

She didn't dare look at him as she asked, "Nicci showed me a scar on her side. She said you tried to kill her."

He sighed. "It's true. But would you have believed me if I told you it was self-defense? Do you even believe me now?"

Georgia hugged herself against the chill of his words. "Why would you—"

"We were out at sea. I'd found some drugs she had hidden and surmised that she'd drugged me to get me to marry her. She'd planned a special supper that night up on deck. I'd seen a motorboat following us at some distance. I just had a bad feeling so I switched the wineglasses at the last minute."

"She tried to drug you again?"

He nodded. "Apparently her plan was to get rid of me at sea. That's why I reacted the way I did when you told me about her marrying someone in Seattle and the husband being lost at sea."

"Why would she do that?"

"Nicci's sick. That's the only thing that explains it."

"Why isn't she in jail? I mean, didn't the police look for her after you told them what had happened on your honeymoon?"

"You have to understand what happened that night," he said. "After I switched the wineglasses, Nicci and I got into it. She threw my glass of wine in my face. I went below to change. She followed me."

Georgia realized she was holding her breath.

"She hadn't consumed enough of the wine for the drug to affect her much. I accused her of tricking me into marrying her. She admitted it. When I glanced in the mirror over the sink, I saw her right behind me." He looked away. "She had a knife in her hand."

NICCI ROSE to her feet and leaned across the kitchen table toward Agnes. "Stop that damned knitting. You're driving me crazy."

"You're already insane."

"This from a demented old woman who doesn't have the sense to know she's about to die?" Nicci gave a rueful shake of her head. "I already told Georgia that you're losing your mind."

"She didn't believe you."

"She will," Nicci said with a smile. "You poor thing. A woman in your condition really shouldn't be living alone. What if you fell down and couldn't get up? Why it might be days before anyone found you."

"Georgia would come looking for me if I didn't show up for knitting class."

"Georgia just puts up with you because you pay her to," Nicci snapped.

"Is that why you're so worried about what I told her about you?" Agnes asked, keeping her tone conversational.

"Georgia is my friend. She wouldn't listen to some addled old woman and anyway, what could you possibly have said to her?"

"Maybe I told her about that night on the ocean when you and your friend tried to kill Dalton Corbett," Agnes said, looking up from her knitting.

Nicci's tanned face paled. "How…?"

"It's the strangest thing," Agnes said. "I was struck by lightning and now I seem to have the *sight*."

Nicci scoffed. "Dalton must have told you." Her eyes widened farther. "Did he tell Georgia?"

"I wouldn't know. I just *saw* it when we shook hands that first day I met you."

"There was something scary about you the moment I met you," Nicci said, looking worried now. "If you would have just eaten that damned cupcake like you were supposed to…"

She reached into her purse, came out with a small, snub-nosed pistol and pointed the barrel at Agnes's head. "This is better though. A nasty fall down your cellar stairs. You really should have been more careful. At least I found you before you laid there for days. Now get up."

"I didn't tell Georgia about that night," Agnes said as she put down her knitting and rose. "Just as I didn't mention it to the sheriff when I called him. I wouldn't want him to think I was getting senile because how could I possibly know anything about your honeymoon?" Agnes cocked her head. "Ah, there's the sheriff now. Right on time."

Nicci's eyes widened in alarm at the sound of a vehicle pulling into the drive. "That can't be the sheriff. Even if you called him when you saw my car, it would take him longer to get here than that."

"It's that annoying *sight*. I knew you were coming plenty ahead of time. So I called the sheriff saying I thought I saw someone out by the barn. After I turned over those poisoned dead birds to him to send to the crime lab, he warned me to let him know if anyone came around the place who I didn't know. Or *trust*," Agnes said and glanced at the gun Nicci was still holding as the sheriff knocked on the front door.

"Come on in, Sheriff, the door's open," Agnes called. "I'd suggest you put that away," she said, dropping her voice.

Angrily, Nicci stuffed the gun into her shoulder bag. Those icy green eyes bored into her. "You say a word to him," she whispered, "and I'll hurt Georgia. And since you have the 'sight,'" she mocked, "you know I can."

"Look who's here, Sheriff," Agnes said as he came into the kitchen. "It's Georgia Michaels's renter. Have you met her? Nicci Corbett meet Sheriff Carter Jackson."

"Agnes told me I could find you here." The sheriff handed Nicci an envelope. "You are duly served, Mrs. Corbett."

"Oh, I'm getting so forgetful," Agnes said, smiling over at Nicci. "When I mentioned to the sheriff that I wanted him to meet you, he said he'd been looking for you. Hasn't this worked out nicely?"

Nicci's face had gone scarlet. She seemed about to say something, but then her cell phone rang.

"You'd better take that," Agnes said. "Something about a sailing school in Seattle, I believe?"

DALTON LOOKED LOST in the past, his face a mask of pain as he stared out at the fair. "I heard the motorboat. I knew it was someone with Nicci and that if I didn't get the knife away from her and get to the shotgun I carried up onboard…"

His gaze came back to Georgia. She looked into his eyes, her heart breaking for him, afraid she already knew what was coming next.

"We wrestled for the knife. If anything, what drug she'd consumed seemed to make her stronger. I finally got the knife from her, but she got away and stumbled up onto deck. I went after her. I could hear the other boat coming alongside. Nicci was waiting for me. She came at me with a fishing gaff and…and I stabbed her."

He took a breath and let it out slowly. "I could see the other boat bobbing in the waves out in the darkness. She screamed, 'Kill him, Ambrose. Kill him,' as I hurriedly got the shotgun. I heard a splash and raced back to where she'd fallen into the water. It was so dark, I couldn't see anything, but I heard the other boat speed off."

Georgia stared at him wide-eyed. "Nicci?"

"I looked for her in the water with a spotlight. I didn't know how badly she was injured, but I knew she was bleeding. When I saw the first shark…" He shook his head. "I thought she was gone. I waited until daybreak, then sailed back toward Galveston planning to go to the police."

"You never saw Ambrose, have no idea who he is?"

Dalton shook his head. "By the time I reached Galveston, I knew I couldn't go to the authorities with my story. Hell, I didn't even believe it and I was *there*. I had no body, no description of Ambrose. The whole story sounded fabricated. I could see myself spending the rest of my life in prison for the death of my wife."

"Well, now you know why this Ambrose never went to the police, either. Nicci *wasn't* dead. He must have gotten her onto his boat when you were going after your shotgun."

He nodded.

"You are so lucky that you figured out what she was up to before…" Georgia shook her head, unable to finish the thought.

"Lucky? I thought I'd killed her. I've lived with the fact that I was capable of killing another human being for the past nine years."

The sun had dipped below the horizon, and the lights on the carnival rides blossomed in the dying light. People began to stream into the fair. The sound of music, clatter of carnival rides and squeals of children drifted on the air along with the scent of corn dogs and cotton candy.

Everything seemed so normal and yet they were sitting under a tree talking about attempted murder.

She squeezed his arm, knowing Nicci's betrayal and his guilt had been slowly killing him. "It was self-defense. You didn't kill anyone."

His gaze locked with hers. "But I *tried* to."

"You had no choice. Who can say what any of us would do under the same circumstances? I'm afraid I would just stand there, too shocked to do a thing. I can't imagine what it must have been like for you, but if you hadn't fought back you wouldn't be here now. Just like her second husband."

"ARE YOU SURE you're all right?" the sheriff asked Agnes after Nicci left.

"Sheriff, I think you should keep an eye on that woman," Agnes said. "She's living over the knitting shop in town. I'm worried about Georgia Michaels. Nicci is a dangerous woman. She cut the brake line on Rory Barrow's pickup in an attempt to kill her and her baby."

"Who told you that?" the sheriff demanded.

Agnes sighed. "It's true but you won't find any proof. The woman covers up her evil too well."

The sheriff rubbed his neck, studying her. "She said she was leaving town. Do you have any reason to believe she'll cause trouble before that?"

Agnes wished she could see the future, but it was as if a black cloud had dropped over her. She could see nothing of the future—only the past and she was exhausted.

Nicci's face had been ashen after she'd taken the call on her cell phone. The conversation had been short.

"Do you have a pen?" Nicci had asked in a strangled voice after snapping the phone shut.

The sheriff had produced one and Nicci had stepped to the kitchen table, ripped open the large manila envelope the sheriff had given her and, ruffling through the pages, found what she was looking for and signed her name.

"Here," she'd said shoving the pen at Agnes. "You witness it."

Agnes had taken the pen, felt a small tremor pass through her, and signed what she knew to be divorce papers. Why Nicci had signed the papers when she'd obviously hadn't wanted to or what all this had to do with a sailing school Agnes couldn't imagine.

That was the problem with her sight. It was just glimpses, no full picture, no clear understanding.

But Agnes's intuition was still working fine. Nicci might have been forced to sign the divorce papers and leave them with the sheriff, but she'd lied about leaving town.

Nicci wasn't through with Whitehorse. Or Georgia. Or even possibly Agnes herself.

"Maybe you could stop by In Stitches and see if Nicci needs helps packing," Agnes suggested now to the sheriff.

Sheriff Jackson smiled. "That would be the neighborly

thing to do, now wouldn't it? Shouldn't you be getting out to the fair to see how your tomatoes did?"

A few days ago, her tomatoes and the fair was all Agnes had been worried about. How things had changed. "I'm heading that way now," she said. "You'll let Georgia know once her tenant is out?"

"I'll make sure Nicci leaves the keys behind."

Agnes patted the handsome sheriff's cheek. "I knew I could depend on you."

DALTON'S CELL PHONE buzzed. He checked it. "I need to take this," he said to Georgia and got to his feet. "Yes?" he said into the phone then listened, his gaze returning to Georgia. "The sheriff is sure? Okay. Thanks. Yeah, that's a huge relief. It's just going to take a while to sink in."

He closed his phone. "Nicci signed the divorce papers and returned them to the sheriff. He caught up with her and followed her to your apartment. After helping her move out of your place, he had Nicci leave the keys on the front counter in your shop."

"She's *gone?*"

"The sheriff said she drove out of town." Dalton sat down and leaned back against the tree trunk again. "I can't believe this. It's too good to be true. She's out of your apartment. Once the paperwork is filed, Nicci will no longer be my wife." He broke into a smile. "Lantry said the sheriff is checking into the bigamist charges and possible wrongful death of her second husband."

"I feel like a huge weight has been lifted off my shoulders."

He laughed. "Now it's in the sheriff's hands," Dalton said, looking as relieved as Georgia felt.

But still she felt skeptical that Nicci would ever be

caught on any charges. Nicci seemed to cover her tracks too well. If they were right, Nicci had gotten away with attempted murder twice that they knew of and murder at least once. And she was still out on the street, free.

Georgia couldn't help but think of that woman she'd met that first day in her shop and took upstairs to see the apartment for rent. It was hard to see her hurting anyone.

What would cause Nicci to do the terrible things she'd done? She'd tried to hurt Rory and the baby. Georgia couldn't forgive her for that and yet her heart went out to the insecure woman she'd glimpsed in Nicci, a woman crying out for help both literally and figuratively.

Nicci would soon be getting the help she needed—locked up where she couldn't hurt anyone else.

"Come on," Dalton said, taking Georgia's hand as he jumped to his feet. "If this doesn't call for a celebration, I don't know what does."

It felt too early to celebrate. Or maybe that was just Georgia's silly superstitious self talking. But when she looked into Dalton's oh-so-blue eyes, Georgia couldn't have denied him anything. He was free, not only from his marriage to Nicci but free of the belief that his actions had led to her death. The man deserved to celebrate.

"What did you have in mind?" Georgia asked, smiling at him.

"You'll see." He grabbed her hand and drew her through the dark toward the bright lights of the carnival.

AGNES STOPPED by the garden division. Her tomatoes had taken the blue ribbon. She tried to feel some joy in that. Her husband would have been proud.

As she walked down to the 4H barn to help finish putting up the displays, all she could do was worry that

Nicci was even more dangerous now—and hadn't left town at all.

She'd been volunteering at the fair for the past fifty years and wasn't about to change that now. She tried to lose herself in her work, pleased to be taking part in another county fair and telling herself there was nothing else she could do.

She was alone in one of the smaller fair buildings displaying some of the needlework when she felt her skin crawl.

Turning, she found Nicci standing directly behind her.

"My mother used to do needlepoint," Nicci said, studying the work Agnes had just hung. "I tried to finish one of hers. How tedious and boring. I can't imagine why she did it."

"Some people say it relieves stress."

Nicci scoffed at that. "Maybe it's why she killed herself."

"I thought you'd left town," Agnes said as she resumed hanging the artwork. She was sure that Nicci had waited until the other volunteers had left before coming in here.

"Leave without saying goodbye to my friends?" Nicci chuckled. "What kind of person would I be if I did that?"

Agnes wasn't about to touch that one.

"You really aren't afraid of me, are you?"

Agnes had never been more afraid of anyone in her life. Nicci was evil on earth. Anyone who wasn't afraid was crazy.

But when she spoke, she said, "I'm an old woman. I've had a good life. I'm not afraid of dying nor of Judgment Day," which was all true.

"You're afraid for your friend Georgia, though, aren't you?" Nicci said, sneering.

Terrified. But Agnes knew better than to show it. She wished she was young and strong and could overpower this woman. But even as she thought it, she knew it would take more than that. It would be a fight to the death.

Agnes prayed that Georgia would be up to it because she feared that would be how it would end for her friend.

"You are going to do whatever it is you do," Agnes said, trying to sound bored. "You're a miserable person who likes to spread that misery around."

Agnes felt Nicci's clawlike hand clamp down on her shoulder. Pain radiated through her shoulder and down her back. She let out a cry as Nicci increased the pressure, less from the pain than from the image that flashed in her mind.

"Agnes?" a woman called from the other side of one of the partitions. Agnes hadn't heard the volunteer return. "Are you all right?"

Nicci let go and Agnes straightened. "Just my arthritis," Agnes managed to say, her voice breaking a little, her eyes brimming with tears. She didn't want Nicci to hurt the other woman and it was something Nicci just might do out of meanness.

"Well, don't over do," the woman called back. "Take a break. Rosie should be coming over to help you anytime now."

Agnes rubbed her shoulder and realized that Nicci was no longer behind her. Where had she gone? Agnes had a very bad thought. Earlier she'd seen Georgia talking with Dalton over by some large cottonwood trees at the edge of the fairgrounds.

"I think I *will* take a break," Agnes called to the other woman and hurried outside. Digging out her cell phone, first she called the sheriff and told him Nicci hadn't left town. He said he'd come out to the fairgrounds and pick her up since there was now an APB out on her for questioning in the death of her second husband and pending bigamy charges.

She tried Georgia's cell and left a message to call.

Failing that, she went to find Georgia and warn her before Nicci found her.

Agnes was even more worried now that she knew how Nicci's mother had died.

Chapter Twelve

"Carnivals make me feel like a kid again," Dalton said, laughing as he bought tickets for the two of them. "Let's ride the Ferris wheel!"

Georgia glanced upward and shuddered.

"If there is something else you'd rather ride…?"

"No," she said, seeing his disappointment. "It looks like fun." She glanced up and quickly looked away.

"Yes?"

She smiled, feeling a shiver of excitement and apprehension, the Ferris wheel evoking the same emotions she felt when she was around Dalton. "Yes."

As they joined the line, Dalton said, "I know what we need. Stay here," he said and ran over to buy them cotton candy.

She laughed as she took a bite. They shared it as they loaded into the chair. The moment the wheel started to turn Georgia gripped the bar that held them in, knuckles turning white.

"Ah, don't tell me you're afraid of heights," Dalton said, shoving back his Stetson to gaze at her.

She swallowed and nodded as the chair rose and other riders loaded. Georgia wasn't afraid of heights, she was terrified of them. She already felt no longer earthbound and with each rock of the chair, she had to clamp down on the cry that wanted to escape her lips.

"It's okay," Dalton said, putting his arm around her. "Don't look down. Look out over the fair. Isn't the view amazing?"

She nodded and loosened her grip a little as their chair began to rise more smoothly. His arm around her felt comforting and the view really *was* something. Hadn't she dreamed of being in Dalton's arms? Just not like this.

They reached the top and she felt the breeze stir her hair. It did feel good up here, cooler, not so bad after all, Georgia thought, until she made the mistake of looking down as they began their descent. She thought she might be sick.

"Georgia?"

When she looked over at him high in the air over the fairgrounds, Dalton thumbed away a spot of cotton candy at the corner of her mouth, his eyes locking with hers and she knew he was about to kiss her. This was definitely not how she'd dreamed it.

"I don't think—"

He touched a finger to her lips. "A part of me died that night at sea. But tonight, here with you, I feel as if I've been given a second chance to live again. For so long nothing has mattered. Georgia, *this* matters. *You* matter."

The chair rocked and he pulled her closer. She relaxed in his arms, leaning into him. The kiss was like the taste of summer, sweet and filled with the scents of the carnival. He enveloped her and she lost herself in the wondrous feel of his mouth on hers, feeling safe, forgetting where she was.

All around them the sounds and sights of the carnival and fair seemed to freeze as if she and Dalton were the only two people left in the world.

AGNES WORKED her way through the crowds toward the tree where she'd seen Georgia and Dalton earlier. Georgia had to still be here. She planned to come out to the fair this evening for the official opening. There'd been no answer at both the shop phone or Georgia's cell, something that worried Agnes.

Was it possible that Nicci had already found Georgia?

How was it that she could sense some things and not others? Not one to question either blessings or curses, Agnes made her way to the cottonwood trees at the edge of the fairgrounds only to find no one around. As she started back across the fairgrounds, she happened to look in the direction of the carnival rides.

Her feet faltered under her and she almost stumbled and fell as she spotted not only Georgia, but Dalton Corbett—on the Ferris wheel. Wasn't Georgia afraid of heights? And how, pray tell, did she know that? Agnes asked herself.

"Doesn't matter," she muttered. "Not my place to question any of it." Although she had to wonder why an old woman like herself had been given this gift.

She started toward the Ferris wheel, keeping the two in sight, planning to be waiting for them at the bottom when they got off so she could warn them that Nicci was here at the fair.

Agnes had only taken a few steps when she saw Nicci. The evil blonde was standing in the shadow of one of the buildings, her gaze pointed upward at the Ferris wheel. It was the hatred in Nicci's expression that stopped Agnes cold.

"Oh, dear," she muttered under her breath as she shot a glance in the direction of the Ferris wheel. Georgia was in Dalton's arms and they were kissing, and Nicci had seen the whole thing.

WHEN THE RIDE ENDED, Georgia pulled back, their chair rocking wildly before it came to a stop. Dalton looked into her gold-flecked brown eyes, losing himself for a long moment. All he wanted to do was kiss her again.

But lifting the bar, he helped her off and saw that her legs were wobbly from the ride. Or from the kiss? He felt a little lightheaded himself.

Their equilibrium barely restored, they were swallowed up in the crowd. Dalton thought he heard someone call to them, but Georgia didn't seem to notice and he didn't see anyone in the crowd he recognized.

"I apologize for that," he said as they worked their way through the throngs of people.

"No, the kiss was…"

"I meant the Ferris wheel ride," he said with a grin.

She smiled shyly. "I enjoyed the ride, really. I'm sorry but I have this thing about heights."

"You *have* ridden a Ferris wheel before, right?"

She shook her head. "But I'm glad my first time was with you."

He laughed and took her hand, touched that she'd agreed to the ride with him—even though she was afraid of heights. They walked through the carnival, lights, sounds and people all around them.

"I meant what I said up there above the fairgrounds," he said quietly as they worked their way through the crowd. His gaze met hers. "I've had the most fun with you that I've ever had."

"Me, too."

As he looked into her eyes, he felt his heart kick up a beat. He wanted this woman. The thought surprised him since he'd thought he'd never feel this way after Nicci.

Nicci. For a while this evening, he'd forgotten about her.

Just because she'd signed the divorce papers and left the keys to Georgia's apartment didn't mean she was really gone from his life. Or from Georgia's.

"I don't think you should go back to your apartment tonight," he said.

"But I thought the sheriff said Nicci was gone."

He brushed a lock of hair back from her face. "I think you should come home with me so I can make love to you."

So HE COULD make love to her? The night had taken on a kind of magic of its own and Georgia felt swept up in it. She'd never ridden a Ferris wheel before or been kissed by a handsome cowboy who made her see fireworks and feel safe so far above the ground.

But that wasn't what had her heart racing. Dalton made her feel adventurous and carefree. In his arms, she felt desire and passion. She wanted to throw caution to the wind, be reckless.

The problem was that she'd always prided herself on being levelheaded. It had gotten her this far. "Thank you for the invitation, but…"

"I'm sorry, that was out of line. We barely know each other." His gaze locked with hers. "That isn't true, is it?"

She shook her head as he stepped toward her, backing her against the warm side of one of the buildings. He touched her face, his blue eyes lit with a fire that ignited her blood and quickened her pulse. She wanted this man who talked to horses, who touched her with hands callused from hard labor, who loved carnival rides and cotton candy.

Georgia cupped his jaw and tilting toward him, softly kissed his lips. She was a woman who'd never played the lottery, never broke the speed limit, never trusted her heart to a man. She'd never even been tempted before.

Follow your heart.

Just this once.

"Yes," she whispered against his lips. "But first I promised I'd stop by the produce exhibit and see Agnes."

DALTON WAS ON HIS WAY to his pickup to wait for Georgia when his cell phone vibrated. He pulled it out, saw who it was from and almost didn't take the call.

"I thought you'd left town," he said, skipping hello.

Nicci laughed. "Who says I haven't? I just called to tell you that you can't have her."

"I don't know what you're talking about." But of course he did.

"I should have known you'd fall for her. Georgia's the type of woman who makes men want to protect her. She makes you want to play hero and save her, doesn't she? The kind of girl a man wants to marry."

He didn't bother to deny it.

"But it isn't going to happen."

"Don't you get tired of playing games with people's lives?"

"No, actually. What else do I have?"

"You have Ambrose," he said.

"Yes, Ambrose."

"What do you have on him anyway?" Dalton asked.

"Isn't it possible that someone loves me just for me?" Her tone was sharp as if the question hurt her.

"You call that *love?*"

"You don't know anything about it. What Ambrose and I have… I didn't call to talk about Ambrose. Maybe I just wanted to say goodbye."

Not likely. "Goodbye."

"And tell you something you need to know," she added before he disconnected. "You might be the only man I ever truly loved, Dalton."

"If you expect me to believe—"

"I came to Whitehorse to kill you, but I couldn't do it. That should prove what I'm saying."

"Am I supposed to thank you?" he asked, unable to hide his irritation. More games.

"But you can't have Georgia," Nicci said. "Don't even try. You're mine. Till death do us part, remember?"

"How could I remember? You drugged me. No more games, Nicci. You and I are divorced. The authorities know about the bigamy out in Seattle. The cops are looking into your husband's death. It won't be long and you'll be behind bars."

"I wouldn't count on that, Dalton. Just as I wouldn't count on us not seeing each other again." The phone went dead.

He stood for a moment gripping it in his fist. A chill rushed up his spine. Hurriedly, he glanced around unable to fight off the feeling that Nicci was close by watching him. She hadn't called to say goodbye.

Georgia.

He took off at a run toward the produce exhibit building, praying he found her before Nicci did.

AGNES WASN'T IN the produce exhibit building. One of the women told Georgia that she'd taken a break.

After learning that Agnes's tomatoes had taken blue ribbons again this year, she moved toward the door to look for Agnes, knowing she wouldn't have taken a very long break.

The first night of the fair seemed unusually busy.

Georgia recognized a lot of people in the crowd, but not everyone. Visitors came from all around this part of Montana.

Getting out of the way of those entering the produce exhibit, Georgia stepped to the side of the building. It seemed cooler here in the dark between the buildings, away from all the people.

"Enjoy the Ferris wheel ride?"

Georgia felt as if she'd seen a ghost as Nicci stepped from the darkness. It took a moment for her to realize what Nicci had said. She'd seen her and Dalton on the Ferris wheel. Had she seen him kiss her? Seen her in his arms?

Georgia took a step back, her heart pounding from shock and fear. Nicci had closed the distance between them, cutting her off from the fair visitors. With the sounds of the carnival rides and the screams and yells of the people on them, even if Georgia called for help, her cries couldn't be heard back here. She was alone with a murderess.

Nicci smiled as if realizing the same thing. "I couldn't leave without saying goodbye to you. After all you're the only friend I had here."

"I'm glad you found me," Georgia said, trying to keep her voice even. "I need to give you back your deposit and last month's rent."

Nicci waved that off. "It's just money. I have so much I'll never be able to spend it all. I'm talking about something much more important. Friendship. You saved me that first day I got to Whitehorse. You befriended me when I had no one. I told you I would never forget it. I owe you."

"That's crazy." The moment the word was out, Georgia cringed, wishing she could pull it back. "I was happy to help you."

"I know, but then I involved you in my divorce. I really

am sorry about that. If it wasn't for me, you might never have met Dalton." Her green eyes seemed to glow in the darkness. "I saw the look on your face that day you came back from his ranch. You said he didn't say anything to you, but I knew that he had. Do you know how much you hurt me?"

"I never meant to hurt you."

"Maybe not, but how could you believe him and not me? I'm sorry I got so upset, but I could see that he was coming between us and I couldn't let that happen."

Just as she couldn't let Rory come between them.

"If it had been Rory you would have believed her over some man."

"Nicci—"

"You were the only friend I had here. I just don't understand how you could turn against me like you have."

Georgia shook her head, unsure what to do, let alone what to say.

"You're not wearing the sweater I bought you."

The swift change of subjects threw Georgia for a moment. "I—"

"Do you know how much time I spent looking for the perfect sweater for you? I knew that color would look beautiful on you. The pale yellow brings out the highlights in your hair."

Georgia flinched as Nicci touched her hair.

"You act as if you're afraid of me."

"Why don't I write you a check for—"

"I told you this isn't about money," Nicci snapped. "It's about loyalty. Betrayal. You were my *best* friend."

"Nicci, you need help."

She laughed. "I'm fine. It's the people who go behind my back and betray me that need help."

Georgia thought she heard the sound of a siren headed

this way. She cocked her head to listen and saw that Nicci was listening as well.

"Dalton is all wrong for you," Nicci said quietly. "I'm telling you for your own good. It's not that I'm jealous. I know that Dalton can't be trusted. I trusted him. Just like I trusted you, but you both disappointed me."

"I'm sorry, Nicci."

"No, you're not. You just want me to go away."

The sound of the sirens died off as the patrol cars pulled into the fairgrounds.

"It isn't going to work, the two of you," Nicci said shaking her head ruefully. "Now you're both going to be sorry. Sorrier than you can know."

Georgia turned at a sound behind her. Agnes appeared out of the dark shadows. She carried a long-handled shovel that was almost as big as she was.

"Agnes, no," Georgia said, turning around, afraid of what Nicci might do when she saw the little elderly woman with a weapon.

When she swung back around though, Nicci was gone.

GEORGIA AND DALTON rode with his pickup windows down, the cool summer night air blowing in the scents of summer. Country-Western songs played on the radio as the truck sped along under a midnight-blue canopy dotted with stars and a sliver of the white moon.

From the moment, he'd found her and Agnes, he hadn't let her out of his sight. They'd both tried to talk Agnes into coming with them, but she'd insisted on staying at the fair, saying Nicci was gone and she would be fine.

Dalton pulled Georgia closer in the cab of the pickup as if they were teenagers on a date, as if still afraid of what might have happened in between the two fair buildings if Agnes hadn't shown up with a shovel.

"Did Nicci threaten you?" he had demanded.

"No, she… It isn't important." She hadn't wanted to spend any more time talking about Nicci. Anyway, Nicci hadn't said anything that she hadn't said before.

The deputies hadn't found her, but Sheriff Jackson had promised they would continue to search for Nicci.

"There is no way I'm letting you go back to your apartment tonight even if you've changed your mind about coming home with me," Dalton had said.

Georgia hadn't been able to help herself. She'd smiled at him, touching his cheek, looking into those amazing blue eyes of his. "I haven't changed my mind."

Now she felt as if they were trying too hard to put the incident behind them as they sang along with the radio, not sounding half-bad together.

She sneaked a look at him as he sang and felt her heart do that little dip it had done at the top of the Ferris wheel. Was it possible to fall in love so quickly?

A week ago she would have said no. Absolutely not.

But now… She felt as close to him as anyone she'd ever known. When she used to question her nana about love and marriage, she always told Georgia not to concern herself about it.

"You'll know when it happens," Nana had said with a laugh. "There's no mistaking the real thing. You're a sensible girl. You'll be able to tell."

She didn't feel terribly sensible right now.

"Having second thoughts?" Dalton asked as he pulled in beside his cabin and cut the engine and lights.

"No," she said and felt herself tremble in his embrace.

He chuckled. "Come on," he said, pulling her out of the pickup.

"Where are you taking me?" she asked when he walked right past his cabin.

"The main house. There's a guest bedroom you can stay in tonight. In the morning we can go get your truck and then I'm taking you to the shop to make sure Nicci isn't hanging around."

"Dalton?" She pulled him to a stop. "I don't understand." But she thought she did as their gazes locked under the starlight.

He took her shoulders in both of his palms. "I still am dying to make love with you. But it has to be when it's right." He touched a finger to her lips. "It isn't right, not tonight, and I don't want to spoil it. I don't want it to be just one crazy night after cotton candy and a Ferris wheel ride at the fair."

And Nicci. Those were the unsaid words that hung between them.

She swallowed, tears welling in her eyes as she gazed gratefully at him. She stepped to him and kissed him quickly. "You do know me, don't you?"

He nodded. "Come on before I weaken and change my mind."

Kate, the night owl, was still up reading in the library.

"I offered Georgia the guest bedroom," Dalton said. "I didn't think you'd mind."

"Not at all," Kate said giving them both a knowing look. "I'll show Georgia where it is."

Dalton leaned over and gave Georgia a kiss. "Good night," he said. "Good night, Kate," he added with a grin.

Both women laughed as he left.

"Another moment and he would have changed his

mind," Kate said. She put her arm around Georgia as they walked down the hall. "So how was the fair?"

They talked for a while about the fair, then Kate showed her where everything was that she might need for the night and gave her a cotton nightgown to sleep in.

"Let me know when your next knitting class begins," Kate said as she left the room. "It's time I learned to knit. Sleep well."

"Thank you," Georgia said, warmed by the woman's generosity.

Kate walked down the hall to the bedroom. Grayson had awakened saying he'd heard voices. "Do we have company?"

"Just an overnight guest," Kate said as she slid in beside her husband and smiled to herself. She wouldn't be surprised if there wasn't going to be another Corbett wedding before very long.

DALTON KNEW he'd done the right thing. That didn't help much on the walk back alone to his cabin. As he climbed the porch steps, he saw the note stuck on his door and feared for a moment it might be from Nicci.

He opened the door, turned on the light and ripped open the note. To his surprise, it was from Lantry. "The sheriff called earlier and wanted you to know that Nicci was spotted in Wolf Point, headed east. Thought that might help you sleep a little better tonight."

Dalton stood there in the doorway, the light spilling out across the porch. Nicci spotted in Wolf Point. That was miles from Whitehorse. Was it possible she was really gone? He wanted to cheer. He wanted to wake up Georgia. Hell, wake up the whole household. His father would make margaritas and Juanita would bring out that wonderful salsa of hers.

But as he glanced back at the main house and saw that all the lights were out, he decided it could wait until tomorrow. Tomorrow, after he was sure that Nicci really was gone. He was just thankful that he'd talked Georgia into staying out here tonight where she was safe. Nicci was crazy, but she wasn't crazy enough to come out here after either of them.

Earlier tonight when he'd been looking for Georgia, he'd seen a man standing in the shadows and been reminded again of Nicci's accomplice, Ambrose. While that man turned out just to be waiting for his wife and kids to finish their carnival rides, Ambrose might still be in Whitehorse.

The patrolman who'd picked Nicci up in Tennessee should be back to work soon. Dalton was anxious to get a description of Ambrose. He would ask his brother to check and see if Nicci had been traveling alone when she'd been spotted in Wolf Point.

Wasn't it possible that by morning, Nicci could be apprehended along with her accomplice?

He recalled their earlier conversation. What had Nicci said? Something like, "Right, I have Ambrose." But did she still? No one had ever stayed around Nicci long. Possibly even this Ambrose fellow had gotten enough of her after Nicci's arrest in Tennessee.

As Dalton stepped into his cabin, he did something he'd only done since Nicci had arrived in town. He locked the door behind him. Trying to put Nicci out of his mind, he let himself think of Georgia Michaels, smiling to himself as he did. How ironic that it was Nicci who had brought them together.

He could well imagine what Nicci must think of that.

Chapter Thirteen

The shop felt strangely empty as Georgia entered it and glanced toward the stairs to the apartments.

"You all right?" Dalton asked, standing next to her.

She nodded, a lump in her throat. It was hard not to remember the first day she'd met Nicci. She'd known then that Nicci was different from anyone she'd ever met. She just hadn't known *how* different.

"We should probably check the apartment," Dalton said and started up the stairs.

Georgia picked up Nicci's keys where the sheriff had left them and followed behind Dalton up. Handing him the key, he opened Nicci's apartment door. How long would she think of the apartment as Nicci's, Georgia wondered as they stepped in.

A cool breeze rustled the curtains at the open window. Dalton stepped to it and looked down at the street before closing the window and locking it.

"Everything here that should be?" he asked Georgia.

She glanced around the immaculate apartment unable to forget Nicci's excitement when she'd first seen it. She'd noticed all the small things Georgia had done.

Shaking her head, she stepped to the bedroom and saw

the empty closet. A shiver ran through her as she remembered the day she'd searched it and found the dry-cleaning bag.

Dalton checked the bathroom and then turned toward her. "Looks as if she didn't leave anything behind. Are you all right?" he asked stepping to her.

She could only nod. Nicci had blown into her life on a whirlwind and blown out just as dramatically. Was she really gone?

"I think you should stay out at the ranch until Nicci is caught," he said, looking as if he wanted to touch her but was afraid for some reason.

Georgia shook her head. She didn't have much faith in the police catching Nicci quickly or possibly ever. She wasn't going to hide out until then.

"I have knitting classes to get ready for," she said. "I worked too hard for this shop to give it up now. This is my *home*. Nicci is gone, and if she isn't," she said quickly before he could interrupt, "she left her keys. She can't get back in. I'll keep the doors locked."

Dalton looked as if he wanted to argue, but he must have seen the stubborn determination in her. "The police will catch her."

Georgia didn't argue the point because she knew it's what he wanted desperately to believe, just as she did. But she wondered if the police would be able to hold Nicci— let alone convict her of anything.

She said as much to Dalton and saw his expression change. He stepped to the window and looked out again. She could see the strong muscles of his back bunch.

"There's something I haven't told anyone. A secret Nicci told me that night on the boat."

Georgia found herself holding her breath.

"She told me that she killed her mother and made it look

like a suicide." He turned from the window. "I didn't believe her. But my reaction to even her saying such a thing made her angry. She said I was the only one she'd ever told and that she thought she could trust me because we were married."

"You think that's why she tried to kill you that night?"

He shrugged. "Maybe. Still, she had Ambrose following us in another boat so who knows what Nicci had planned?"

"Isn't it possible that she *did* love you? That she told you because she didn't want any secrets between you? A test to see how you took it?"

Dalton's blue eyes widened. "You might be right. That's what she said that night. I said sure, but I had no idea…"

Georgia hugged herself against the cold chill that snaked around her even though the room was warm from the morning summer sun. "She confessed to you. Isn't it possible she's worried that you're the only person left alive who knows the truth?"

"WELL, AT LEAST that might answer one question," Lantry said later at Trails West Ranch. "She showed up in White-horse to see how much of a threat you were to her."

Dalton studied the outline of the Little Rockies in the distance from his cabin porch. He thought about what Nicci had said about coming here to kill him and then changing her mind. He'd thought she was just playing games with him. Was it possible she'd been telling the truth?

It had been almost a week now. There had been another sighting of Nicci in Minnesota. He was getting to the point where he wasn't looking over his shoulder anymore.

For the first few days, he'd stayed so close to Georgia that he'd become her shadow.

"Dalton, we have to stop this," she'd finally said after

he'd insisted on sleeping in the apartment across the hall and had even hung around some of her knitting classes during the day. "Nicci is gone. Probably to some country that doesn't extradite."

With Nicci's money she could go anywhere in the world. Getting a passport in another name would be child's play for her.

"The sheriff says there's enough circumstantial evidence to arrest her," Dalton said now to his brother.

"How many dead husbands have they found?"

"Five so far. All men who took sailing lessons from Nicci and died at sea on their honeymoons. She used that husband's name until she remarried. That's how she disappeared. The FBI is still investigating."

Lantry shook his head. "You were damned lucky."

Didn't Dalton know it.

"What do you think makes her do it?" his brother asked.

He shrugged. "Maybe she is looking for someone who loves her in spite of who she is." He shook his head. That was as close as he would ever come to understanding Nicci.

"What about this Ambrose? He must love her in spite of who she is. Or more likely because of it."

"If he's still with her. He didn't show here in Whitehorse. They could have parted company back in Tennessee after Nicci's arrest."

"Or she could have gotten rid of him. Damn, I haven't heard back about Ambrose from that highway patrolman in Tennessee. He's got to have returned from vacation now. He and his family were some place out in the wilderness without cell phone coverage." Lantry chuckled. "People in the cities don't believe there is still such a place."

"Only because they haven't been to Whitehorse,"

Dalton said. "A mile out of town and there's no coverage until you reach Lewistown, two hours to the south."

"I'll call and get that information on Ambrose for you," Lantry said pulling out his cell. "I left a message for him to call me."

Dalton hoped the day came soon when he never had to hear either the names Nicci and Ambrose again. "I just want to put this behind me."

His brother nodded and pocketed his phone again. "Well, you got your divorce so now you're free to see all you want of your knit-shop girl."

Dalton wished it were that simple. He feared that all he did was remind Georgia of Nicci. "I'm giving it a little time. She's been through a lot."

"You're waiting for Nicci to be caught," Lantry said and swore under his breath. "What if she's never caught?"

Dalton shook his head. He had no answer. All he knew was that he felt it was better to cool things with Georgia for a while.

"Damn it, Dalton, you've let Nicci mess with your mind for the last nine years. How many more years are you going to give this woman?"

He didn't know. He kept remembering her words to him that night at the fair. You can't have her. *You can't have Georgia. Don't even try. You're mine. Till death do us part, remember?*

Maybe Nicci really had spared his life because she loved him. But if she thought for a moment that he might find happiness with Georgia... Well, there was no doubt in his mind that even with the entire country's law enforcement officers and the FBI looking for her, Nicci would come back to make sure he never had Georgia—just as she'd promised.

As THE DAYS WENT BY, Georgia felt Dalton pulling away. While she hadn't wanted him guarding her 24/7, she missed the fact that he hardly ever stopped by the shop anymore. He still called occasionally, but they were so busy avoiding talking about Nicci that their conversations ended quickly.

Georgia had hoped once Nicci was caught that they might be able to put her out of their lives. Nicci seemed to have dropped off the face of the earth. Rory worried that she had found a job at another sailing school and was now picking out her next husband to kill.

Just the thought sent terror coursing through her. She'd had Nicci living right here until her roof. Georgia knew how lucky she'd been, but wished the sheriff had been able to confirm some of the charges against Nicci before she'd escaped.

This morning Georgia had finally put the Apartment for Rent sign back in the front window. For a while, she'd thought about not renting the apartment at all. But she needed the money and maybe having someone else in there would help ease Nicci's memory.

As her knitting class filed in, Rory getting bigger by the day, Agnes patted Georgia's hand.

"You look as if you aren't getting much sleep, dear," Agnes whispered. "Perhaps you should stay with your friend Rory for a while."

"I'm fine," Georgia tried to reassure her. Agnes looked as if she hadn't gotten much sleep herself. "Are you all right out there on the farm by yourself?"

Agnes chuckled. "I've been on that farm for more than fifty years. I plan to die there. So don't you be worrying about me."

Georgia had smiled and class had begun. She'd kept

busy enough that her mind hadn't wandered too much. Agnes had brought her some fresh vegetables from her garden and one of her other students had given her a box of chocolates for her help unraveling some of her knitting.

Rory stayed for a few minutes after class was over. "The doctor said I could deliver any day. I'm so hot and miserable, boy am I ready."

Georgia laid a hand on her friend's stomach and smiled. "He sure is kicking up a storm today. Feels as if he's ready to break out."

Rory laughed. "He has been more active than usual today. Maybe." She crossed her fingers.

"You call me, no matter what time of the day or night. I have Miss Thorp standing by for shop duty."

Rory hugged her as best she could. "How are you doing?"

"Fine."

"No, really. You look a little peaked, as my mother used to say." Rory studied her. "It's Dalton. I know that look."

"He seems to have really backed off."

"He's afraid if he gets involved with you and Nicci finds out…"

Georgia shook her head. "I can't live my life that way."

"Have you told him that?"

"No, but—"

"No buts about it. Tell him. You two need to talk. You can't let Nicci ruin the rest of your lives. She is probably living it up on a sailboat in some tropical sea and not giving a thought to either of you."

Georgia could only hope.

"Call him. Invite him over for supper. Cook up some of Agnes's wonderful vegetables. Talk."

"Thank you."

"What for? I didn't offer to cook," Rory joked.

"You are the best friend anyone could ever have."

THE INVITATION HAD come out of the blue. "Supper? Tonight?" Dalton searched around for a reason to decline, then mentally kicked himself. "Sure."

"I think we need to talk," Georgia said.

He'd been avoiding her. But he'd thought that best under the circumstances. Just the sound of her voice made him sorry he'd done that. If Nicci wanted to make their lives miserable she didn't need an excuse. And it wasn't as if she was hiding out in town watching them.

"Great. What can I bring?"

"Just yourself. Agnes dropped by some fresh vegetables from her garden this morning before class and a friend gave me some walleye fillets from Nelson that I thought would be good."

His heart soared at the happiness he heard in her voice. "You're making my stomach growl. What time?"

"How about seven? I'm really looking forward to this."

"Me, too. I'll see you then. Georgia? Thanks for calling." He hung up more excited about this date than any he'd ever been on.

Georgia couldn't contain her excitement. Rory had been right. Asking Dalton to supper had been a good idea. She could still hear the pleasure in his tone.

She had taken Rory's advice and was planning to cook the fresh vegetables Agnes had brought her. They wouldn't take long to cook. Nor would the walleye fish fillets she would fry.

Georgia had even bought a bottle of wine. What had gotten into her? She was half hoping they wouldn't get to supper and felt her face heat at the thought and her heart race.

In the distance she heard the rumble of thunder. Another summer storm. She hoped it rained and cooled things down. Her apartment felt a little too warm. Or maybe it was just thinking about tonight that had her temperature soaring, she thought with a nervous laugh.

When she heard someone on the stairs, she glanced at her watch, surprised Dalton was early. He must be as anxious as she was, she thought as she checked herself in the mirror and started toward the door.

She stopped halfway across the room as she heard a key in the apartment door lock. She'd left the back door open downstairs for Dalton. He'd promised to lock it before coming up. Now someone was turning a key in the lock of her apartment door.

Georgia stood glued to the spot as her mind raced. No one had a key to her apartment. She'd thought about giving one to Rory, but she'd known her friend would never be able to find it if she needed it. So who could be—

The door swung open and Georgia heard the slight tinkle of silver bracelets an instant before she saw the woman framed in the doorway.

AGNES WOKE from her nap with a start. She'd been dreaming about her husband and wanted to cling to the dream rather than wake up without him.

She looked around the cool bedroom, wondering what had awakened her. Wind blew the curtains into the room. Past them she could see that the late afternoon sky had turned black with thunderheads. As a bolt of lightning splintered the sky, Agnes felt the hair on the back of her neck stand on end.

Thunder rumbled over the large old farmhouse. It took her a moment to come fully awake. She'd slept longer and harder than she thought and that worried her only a little.

It wasn't as if she had something she had to do. Her life was her own and had been for years.

Picking up her knitting from where she'd dropped it on the bed, Agnes swung her feet over the side and stood. She was a little hungry. She'd made a nice beef roast earlier with potatoes, carrots, turnips and onions from her garden. Maybe she'd heat some of it up for supper, then watch a little television and knit.

She'd only taken a couple of steps when a thought almost struck her down. She wasn't alone. She froze, listening for the creak of the old wood on the porch as someone moved surreptitiously across it. She heard nothing but the wind whipping the huge old cottonwoods that stood like sentinels around the house. Had she heard a car earlier? She couldn't be sure, she'd been sleeping so soundly…

Agnes clutched her knitting to her as she moved cautiously toward the front of the house to peer out the front window.

She was almost to it, her hand reaching for the curtain to draw it back and peer outside, when she had a flash of dead trash birds followed instantly by a pain in her bruised shoulder in the spot where Nicci had dug in her fingers.

She dropped her knitting as she felt the house go cold.

GEORGIA SUCKED IN A BREATH when she saw the woman standing in her apartment doorway. She'd been so sure it would be Nicci. Her mind had been racing to understand how Nicci could have gotten a key to her apartment.

That day when Nicci had borrowed the pickup. Georgia had handed over her keys. Nicci could have made a copy. Must have.

But the woman standing in her apartment doorway

wasn't Nicci. This woman was tall with long blond hair and looked vaguely familiar.

"What—"

That was all Georgia managed to get out before the woman closed and locked the apartment door behind her.

Georgia took a step back, looking for her cell phone where she'd dropped it on the end table by the couch. "Who are you? What do you want?"

"Take it easy," the woman said, her bracelets tinkling softly as she stepped toward her. "You don't want to do anything you'll regret."

She sounded just like Nicci and she was dressed like her, including the three silver bracelets dangling from her wrist and the tiny silver sailboat necklace around her throat.

A scream caught in Georgia's throat. Screaming would do nothing since all the businesses around her had already closed for the evening and there was little chance anyone would hear her since the main street was empty.

She took a step toward the couch and grabbed up her phone, remembering belatedly that she'd turned the cell off, not wanting to take any calls while Dalton was here for supper.

The woman snatched the phone from her hand. "If you ever want to see Agnes Palmer again, you'll chill, you hear?"

The woman flipped her hair back from her face and Georgia remembered in a flash where she'd seen the woman before.

She'd seen her from the upstairs window when the woman had stopped to ask directions from Nicci. Only the woman hadn't been asking directions.

"Come on, let's go."

"Where are we going?" Georgia asked, edging away from the woman.

"Agnes is waiting for us. If we're late, well, you know Nicci. She doesn't have a lot of patience."

Georgia couldn't stand the thought that Nicci had Agnes and might be hurting her.

"Also Nicci said to be sure and bring that sweater she bought you."

"The sweater? I don't understand. Why are you doing this?"

"Because Nicci asked me to."

Georgia felt terror burrow under her skin. "Who did you say you were?"

"I guess no one told you about me." She seemed amused. "I'm Ambrose."

DALTON KNEW HE WAS EARLY, but he couldn't help himself. He couldn't wait to see Georgia. There was so much he wanted to say to her and he feared if too much more time went by, they might lose each other.

That would be the real tragedy in all this. He felt something deep and abiding for Georgia and sensed she felt it too. If they let Nicci ruin this for them...

Dalton just wasn't going to let that happen, he thought as he studied the dark clouds on the horizon. The air blowing in his side window felt cooler already. He breathed it in and smiled to himself. He felt as if he'd been in limbo for nine years. Georgia had pulled him out of it. She'd shown him what his life could be like and damned if he wasn't ready to fight for her.

From up the road, he spotted a pickup coming toward him and frowned. Georgia?

There must have been a change of plans. But why hadn't she just called? He slowed a little, expecting Georgia to stop, but she sped on past headed south toward Old Town Whitehorse.

Dalton blinked. It *had* been Georgia's pickup and definitely her behind the wheel, but she'd seemed to make a point of not looking at him as she passed him. No way would she not have recognized his truck. Nor had she been alone.

There'd been another woman in the passenger seat. Not Rory. Not Nicci either, he thought with relief. But the other woman *had* been blond. The hair though had been long and straight.

He stopped and swung the pickup around, planning to chase her down and find out what was going on. His cell phone rang. He grabbed it and flipped it open without even bothering to see who was calling he'd been so sure it was Georgia.

"I just heard back from that patrolman in Tennessee," his brother Lantry said when Dalton answered. "I hope you're sitting down. I got a detailed description of Taylor K. Ambrose from the Tennessee patrolman. Taylor K. Ambrose is actually Taylor *Karen* Ambrose. Ambrose is a woman! Tall, blond and beautiful. But wait until you hear this."

Dalton was already swinging the pickup around and heading down the road after Georgia's pickup.

"You wondered what Ambrose's connection was to Nicci?" Lantry was saying. "Well, the patrolman said one of the FBI agents told him that Ambrose is none other than the woman Nicci's father was having the affair with—that's right, the young girl caught in the scandal because she was in the car with Nicholas Angeles the night he died."

Chapter Fourteen

Dalton took off after the pickup. It finally made sense. Nicci and Ambrose. Not another man. A *woman*. The woman who'd taken Nicci's father away from her and somehow the two women had ended up in cahoots? He tried to get his head around that, fighting the fear that came with it.

"Ambrose has Georgia," he said into the phone.

"What?"

"I was on my way into Georgia's for dinner and I saw her pickup headed south. There was a woman with long blond hair in the cab with her."

Lantry swore. "What are you going to do?"

"They're headed south toward Old Town Whitehorse," he said. "Ambrose must be taking her to Nicci. I'm going after her."

Dalton expected his brother to try to talk him into calling the sheriff and was surprised when Lantry said, "Don't call the sheriff. For Nicci to come back here with Ambrose… She has nothing to lose."

He'd been thinking the same thing. Nicci had every law enforcement officer in the country after her, including the FBI. She wouldn't hesitate to kill again.

"She isn't after Georgia," Lantry said. "She wants you."

Dalton was counting on it. He slowed, keeping enough distance between him and the pickup. With luck, Ambrose wouldn't know his truck. That was why Georgia hadn't looked in his direction. The woman was smart and cool-headed. She would be fine. He had to believe that.

The storm moved in. Thunderheads blew across the prairie extinguishing the last of daylight. Dalton saw Georgia turn on her headlights as the first hard drops of rain pinged off his windshield.

He let a rancher in a two-ton truck pass, falling back to put plenty of distance between him and Georgia's pickup. He had no idea what Ambrose would do if she spotted him following them.

Hell, he had no idea what had brought Nicci back to Whitehorse except for a nagging suspicion that had his heart racing.

He could still get glimpses of Georgia's pickup from behind the big ranch truck. Where was Ambrose taking her?

He thought of Lover's Leap, where he'd met Nicci that day. Surely she wasn't going back there. Not on a day like today.

With relief, he watched Georgia turn left toward Old Town Whitehorse instead of right onto the road to the river.

He drove on past the turnoff, following the farm truck. Over the next rise, he stopped and turned around as he considered what was down the road Georgia had taken.

Ranches and farmhouses out here near the Missouri Breaks were few and far between. He knew the road eventually led to Old Town Whitehorse, but he doubted that was where Georgia was headed. She must be holed up in one of the farmhouses along the way. An abandoned one?

He drove back up the road and turned to follow as a burst of lightning illuminated the countryside. Even though the rain was coming down harder now, he could still see a plume of dust Georgia had kicked up in her pickup.

The sky darkened again. Dalton turned off his headlights as he drove down the narrow dirt road, keeping Georgia's taillights in view.

This country was wide and open, rolling hills and vast dark sky. He could see her taillights for miles. But his fear was that she would turn off the road and he might lose her.

His fear was so intense he had trouble catching a breath. If Ambrose had Georgia, where was Nicci?

The pickup's brake lights glowed brighter. Georgia was pulling into the yard of a huge old farmhouse.

He kept going, driving on past, but noting the name on the mailbox: Palmer.

GEORGIA GLANCED in her rearview mirror as Dalton's pickup sped past.

"Is there a problem?" Ambrose asked, glancing over her shoulder at the road behind them.

The pickup kept going, disappearing over a small rise.

"Other than you holding a gun on me?" Georgia asked.

The woman smiled. She reminded Georgia a little of Nicci, a rich girl who'd always had it all.

Georgia looked out through the now pouring rain at the large old farmhouse. Only one lone light flickered from behind the curtains. She felt her heart ache at the thought of Agnes in there with Nicci.

Rain pounded the roof of the pickup and careened off the hood. Lightning flickered all around them, followed almost instantly by nerve-racking booms of thunder.

Georgia was jumpy enough with Ambrose holding a gun on her—and knowing Dalton was somewhere nearby. That had definitely been his truck she'd passed earlier. At the time she'd hoped he'd seen her. He had because he'd just driven past.

But did he know about Ambrose? That she was tall and blond and just as deadly as he'd feared? Georgia had made a point of not checking her rearview mirror before she turned into Agnes's yard, but seeing him drive past just now left her both relieved and afraid. She wasn't entirely alone. But Dalton, she feared, would be in as much danger as she was.

What would he do now?

For that matter, what was *she* going to do?

THE WIND BLEW IN the rain, soaking the flapping curtains. Agnes rushed to the windows to close them, feeling the sting of the drops. She was already chilled just knowing that Nicci was somewhere in the house.

Why hadn't she shown herself?

Agnes's flesh crawled as she shut and locked the last window. The house felt unusually cold and empty. It had always been too large for Agnes and her husband. They'd planned to fill it with children. When that hadn't happened, they'd closed off some of the extra rooms, just as they'd closed off that part of their hearts with regret.

As Agnes started to turn away from the window, a bolt of lightning lit the yard and she saw through the pouring rain the pickup sitting out front.

Her heart dropped at the sight of Georgia's truck. Earlier Georgia had called her to thank her again for the garden vegetables and told her about the dinner she had planned with Dalton Corbett.

"It sounds as if you'll have a wonderful dinner," Agnes had said, giving Georgia her blessing.

After she'd hung up, she'd felt a sense of knowing again. Something horrible had happened at sea on

Nicci's honeymoon with Dalton Corbett. Something that Agnes feared had sealed the two of them together in some awful bond that couldn't be broken until death parted them.

She shivered now, chilled at the thought of what would happen in the next few hours. A deadly cold had settled into the house and into her heart.

Another bolt of lightning daggered down in the dark sky behind the curtain, momentarily blinding her. Thunder boomed and the light Agnes had turned on, blinked off. The power had gone off as it often did out here during storms.

The house went dark, but not so dark that she couldn't see the woman who'd come up behind her. Nicci's hideous smiling face was reflected in the windowpane streaked with rain.

"LOOKS LIKE it's not letting up," Ambrose said over the pouring rain outside of the cab pickup. "You don't mind getting a little wet, do you?" The question was obviously rhetorical as Ambrose reached across and opened Georgia's door. "Don't forget. You do anything stupid and Agnes pays the price."

Georgia wasn't likely to forget. She stepped out, raindrops pelting her with huge icy droplets, as she ran toward the porch.

The front door blew open on a gust of wind. Georgia stumbled into the dark living room, Ambrose behind her still holding the gun.

"Agnes?" Georgia called, fearing that Nicci had already done something to the sweet elderly lady.

"In here," called Agnes from the back of the house. She sounded fine. Maybe Nicci hadn't—

A light blinked on from the kitchen down the hall and

Georgia caught her breath at the sight of Nicci standing silhouetted against it.

She stood, the gun at her side, smiling. "Glad to see you could make it," she said, sounding as if they'd all come out for dinner.

Ambrose pushed Georgia forward, forcing her to walk down the long hallway toward the glow of the lamp and the two women waiting for her.

"The lights went off, but Agnes here is so resourceful, she had a kerosene lantern," Nicci said. "She is just full of surprises."

Ambrose shoved Georgia into one of the kitchen chairs and tossed the pale yellow sweater Nicci had bought her on the table.

"You don't seem all that happy to see me again," Nicci commented before leaning down to give Georgia a quick hug. "I still think of you as a friend despite everything."

She was insane. Georgia wanted to believe that over the alternative—that Nicci was evil on earth.

"What's going on, Nicci?" Georgia asked, surprised she sounded so calm. One look at Agnes and her fear had leaped even higher. She and Agnes both knew why Nicci had come back.

"I just had to tie up some loose ends and I've never seen you in that sweater. Put it on."

"Nicci—"

"Now!"

DALTON'S HEART THUNDERED in his chest as he sprinted over the rise through the rain and saw the shapes of two people melt into the dark shadows of the massive old farmhouse.

He'd caught the glint of a gun in the dim light. Ambrose was armed. That meant Nicci had to be packing as well.

She and her friend were waiting for him. They had Georgia and Agnes. That was all he could think about.

He sprinted toward the farmhouse through the tall green grass. He'd parked in the ditch up the road from the Palmer farmhouse and ran back. He had no weapon, no real plan. All he knew was that somehow he had to save Georgia. He didn't care what happened to him, but he couldn't let Nicci hurt her.

A bolt of lightning illuminated him for an instant before the sky went black again. He cut across a field heading for what looked like a garden, the cornstalks high.

He'd just reached the garden when his cell phone vibrated. He stopped to hunker down in the field of corn and check the caller. Nicci. Just as he'd known it would be.

The phone vibrated again. He tried to catch his breath, needing to be calm and not give himself away. It vibrated a third time. He saw the garden shed off to his right and ran to it, stepping inside before he said, "What do you want?" into the phone.

"I have your lover." Her voice was filled with jubilance.

Dalton forced a laugh. "I don't have a lover."

"Oh? I'm surprised, Dalton. I thought you and Georgia would have consummated your relationship by now. You and I were lovers within hours after we met."

"I'm more cautious now."

"Is that it? Or is it that you think Georgia is special? The kind of woman a man takes home to meet his family?"

The truth in her words made his heart pound a little harder. If Nicci had already figured that out—

"Surely you hadn't planned on waiting until you were married?" She laughed. "I fear you're going to miss out."

"Why are you doing this?" he asked, realizing he actually wanted to know, although he suspected it wasn't even clear in that sick warped mind of hers.

"Do you know I've always regretted that night on the boat?" Nicci asked. "I've thought about it the last nine years and I think we could have made it."

"You kind of crumbed the deal when you tried to kill me, Nicci."

"It wasn't my idea. It was Ambrose—" She broke off. "Too late now, huh. Still I wanted you to know. I loved you." He heard her take a deep breath and let it out. It sounded as if there were tears in voice as she said, "Anyway, I have Georgia."

"She doesn't have anything to do with this, Nicci," he said as calmly as he could manage.

"I think you should come out to Agnes Palmer's place. Think you can find it quickly because I'm really tiring of all this, Dalton. You have forced me to do things that I didn't want to do."

"Nicci, don't—"

But she'd already hung up.

Dalton broke from the cornfield and sprinted toward the back of the house. A sole light flickered from one of the windows. He started up the back steps.

A step creaked under his weight, then another. He moved a little faster, telling himself they wouldn't kill him outright. Nicci was like a cat with a mouse. She would have to bat him around for a while. Tease him. Torment him a while longer before she finally put him out of his misery.

His worry was that she planned to use Georgia to do it.

He reached the back door and grasped the knob.

GEORGIA GLANCED AT AGNES. The elderly woman had been sitting at the table so quietly that Georgia feared Nicci had done something to her before she and Ambrose had arrived.

Agnes's gaze met hers. "What is our next project going to be for knitting class?"

Georgia blinked. Agnes wanted to talk knitting at a time like this? Maybe Nicci had been telling the truth about Agnes starting to lose her mind. "I...I don't know."

"I'm thinking we should make a baby bunting," she said thoughtfully. "All these babies everyone is having."

Nicci shot Agnes a look, then cut her eyes to Georgia as if to say, "Told you so." She turned her back on Agnes, her gun back at her side. Earlier when she'd been on the phone with Dalton, she'd pocketed the gun and had Ambrose keep both Georgia and Agnes in her sights.

Georgia had listened to Nicci's side of the conversation, knowing it was Dalton on the other end of the line.

She tried not to watch the back door or listen too intently for him, for fear Nicci would notice.

But her heart was pounding with anticipation and fear. Ambrose had put her gun in her pocket, but Nicci still had hers and Georgia didn't doubt for a moment that she would use it if Dalton came bursting in.

"I need a glass of water," Agnes said, getting to her feet.

"Sit down!" Nicci ordered.

"I'm thirsty. I always drink eight big glasses of water a day. If I don't—"

"Fine," Nicci snapped. "Ambrose get her some water to shut her up."

"Not that glass," Agnes said. "That big tall thin one. I can't lift those heavy ones anymore."

Nicci motioned with a scowl for Ambrose to get Agnes the other glass. "Now shut up," she snapped when Ambrose put the glass in front of her and Agnes took a sip.

Nicci seemed subdued, almost sad, as they waited.

Georgia feared the reason why. She couldn't get it out

of her head that this is where it would end for all of them. Nicci must just be waiting for Dalton to get here.

"You don't mind if I knit, do you?" Agnes asked.

"Get the old crone her knitting," Nicci ordered Ambrose.

"It's in the living room where I dropped it," Agnes said, sounding bored with all this.

Ambrose disappeared only to return a few moments later with the baby afghan Agnes had been working on.

Agnes pulled out the two needles and ball of yarn, then studied the afghan for a moment. "I'm glad you talked me into these colors, Georgia."

"Oh, shut up, you stupid old woman," Nicci snapped.

In the flickering light of the kerosene lantern, Agnes began to knit as if oblivious to what was taking place in her kitchen.

DALTON KNEW there was no way he could sneak into the house. Nicci was waiting for him. She would have Georgia and Agnes guarded. If he tried to pull something heroic, he could get both of them shot. He had to assume that both Nicci and Ambrose were armed while he had no weapon.

Nicci wanted him. He could only hope for a chance to save Georgia and Agnes, even if it meant taking a bullet himself.

He turned the doorknob, not surprised to find the door wasn't locked.

Nicci turned in surprise, the gun in her hand coming up so the barrel was aimed at his chest. "That was quick."

"This is between you and me," Dalton said, raising his hands as he stepped in. He took a quick glance toward Georgia and Agnes. They sat at the round oak kitchen table. Agnes was knitting and didn't seem to hear him come in. Georgia met his gaze with one of fear for him as Ambrose pulled her gun as well.

"Let Agnes and Georgia go," he said quietly.

"Close the door," Nicci ordered.

He did as he was told.

"And you're wrong. It was *once* between you and me. Back when I thought you were a man to be trusted. I told you my secret and what did you do?"

"You don't think you were asking a lot, Nicci, given the secret you wanted me to keep?"

She actually looked as if she might cry, but the gun in her hand never wavered. "It wasn't my only secret, so if you couldn't accept that one how could you…"

He knew what was coming, had known the moment Lantry told him the name of Nicci's father's lover. Taylor K. Ambrose.

"Accept that Ambrose and I killed my father as well?" Nicci asked simply, but her voice broke at the end. "I *loved* him so much."

"So you kill everything you love?" He saw that now, the poor little rich girl, greedy in her need and easily disappointed in those she loved most.

Nicci glanced back at Ambrose, her expression darkening. "Not everyone." Her gaze came back to him. "I didn't kill you."

"But you damn sure tried," he said, wondering about this strange bond between Nicci and Ambrose. A deadly bond that went back nine years. Was it possible that Ambrose was the only person Nicci ever felt she could trust because of that deadly secret—and apparently no love—between them?

Nicci ratcheted the gun and pointed it at his head. "All secrets die here today. Move over by Ambrose."

Dalton saw the look in her eye and did as she asked. This way he would be closer to Georgia, might be able to shield her. He didn't believe Nicci was ready to kill him. This would have been so not like her to end this quickly, humanely.

"Killing more people is only going to get you executed," he said as he joined Ambrose on that side of the kitchen and Nicci turned, her back to the door.

Dalton thought about making his play now, but Nicci anticipated he might try something. She swung the barrel of her gun toward Georgia.

"The police can't prove anything," Nicci said, swinging the gun to point it at him. "But I couldn't bear to see anyone I cared about get on the stand and tell them my secrets in a way that would make them sound like a confession."

Nicci's eyes narrowed, her trigger finger tightening. Dalton must have blinked, anticipating the intense burn of the bullet as it entered his body.

The blast inside the small room was deafening. He heard a soft, surprised sound come out of Ambrose. He looked over at her shocked face an instant before she dropped, her gun dropping as she hit the floor.

Dalton didn't think. He just dove for the gun, putting his body in front of Georgia. He heard Nicci scream "Don't!" but he already had Ambrose's gun in his hand and was coming up with it.

The sound of the shot seemed far away. He didn't feel the pain, didn't even realize he'd been hit, until he felt his legs give out under him and a sick hot blackness take him to the floor.

GEORGIA SCREAMED and lunged toward Dalton, but Nicci stopped her, slamming the butt of the gun into her shoulder.

She let out a cry and stumbled back. Nicci shoved her down into the chair, the barrel of the gun now pointed between her eyes.

Dalton lay on the floor bleeding. Georgia stared over at him, not daring to move and felt her pulse leap at the sight of his chest rising and falling. Thank God, he wasn't dead. Not yet, anyway.

"I'll reinvent myself after tonight," Nicci said more to herself than to anyone left alive in the room. "I have money stashed all over the world. I'll find another Ambrose." She frowned and for a moment Georgia thought she might cry. "I might even find another Dalton Corbett."

The lantern light flickered over Nicci's face. Georgia saw that her eyes were empty. No soul, she thought with horror.

She didn't see Agnes move, didn't even realize she had until she heard the tumbler of water hit the floor. The thin glass shattered, sending shards flying into the air. Slivers found Nicci's bare ankles and blood bloomed from the tiny cuts.

"You clumsy old hag," Nicci cried and lunged across the table to backhand her. The glancing blow caught Agnes on the cheek and she slumped over onto her knitting without a sound.

Georgia leaped to her feet when she saw Nicci reach across the table to hit Agnes. She lunged for Nicci's arm to stop her, failing, but managing to knock the gun from her hand to the table.

Georgia grabbed the gun and aimed it at Nicci. "Don't move or I'll shoot."

Nicci laughed. "*You're* going to shoot me? Get serious." She took a step toward Georgia. "Didn't you just see what a bullet does when it rips through flesh?"

Georgia took a step back, the weapon wobbling in her hand. She stilled it by clutching the gun in both hands. She heard Agnes moan and saw her lift her head from the table. She looked dazed.

"You've probably never even held a gun before," Nicci was saying. "Wouldn't even know how to fire it, even if you weren't too nice and sweet to pull the trigger and kill someone."

Georgia could hear the truth in Nicci's words. The gun in her hand suddenly felt too heavy. The barrel bobbed. She fought to keep it on Nicci.

"Come on, Georgia, you know you couldn't live with yourself if you took my life." Nicci's smile broadened as she took another step toward Georgia. "That is the difference between us," she said as she lunged for the gun.

Georgia closed her eyes and pulled the trigger.

The sound was deafening in the large kitchen. It echoed off the walls as the gun jerked in Georgia's hand. Nicci let out a cry and clutched her side. Her green eyes darkened. She opened her mouth as if to say something, but no words came out.

Georgia stared at her in horror as Nicci slumped to the floor. The gun dropped from her hand as she stumbled to where Dalton lay bleeding on the floor. She knelt next to him and felt for a pulse. She could hear Agnes get up and go to the phone on the kitchen wall to call the sheriff.

"Tell him we need an ambulance!" Georgia cried.

For a moment, she didn't feel a pulse and felt panic rise in her. Not Dalton. God, no, not Dalton!

Then she felt his blood coursing through his veins. His pulse was weak, but he was still alive. He stirred, his eyes opening, slowly focusing on her face. A smile curled his lips. He whispered something she couldn't hear.

"An ambulance is on the way," she said, listening to Agnes's conversation on the phone behind her. "Don't try to talk. Everything is going to be all right. Just hang in there. Please. I can't lose you. Not now."

He whispered something again she couldn't make out. Bending down, she put her ear closer.

"Nicci."

He was asking about Nicci? "She's—" The rest of her words were lost as she heard the click of the revolver and felt the cold steel pressed into her temple.

Georgia hadn't seen Nicci crawl over to the gun, but Dalton had.

"Say goodbye, Georgia. How perfect. You get to die leaning over your almost lover," Nicci said and laughed.

"Nicci, dear?" The woman had always underestimated her, Agnes thought. Nicci had completely forgotten about her. Behind her, Agnes put down the phone and picked up her knitting from the table.

She'd heard the things Nicci had said to poor Georgia and known them to be true. Georgia wasn't a killer. She would have trouble living with the knowledge if she'd killed someone.

Agnes, though, well, she was old and didn't have that many years to live with *anything*—especially guilt or regret even if she could have felt remorse over killing someone as depraved as Nicci Angeles.

She pulled the needles out of the lovely baby afghan she was making and stepped to where Nicci was crouched with the gun to Georgia's temple.

"Nicci, dear?" she repeated. "I wonder if I might trouble you for a cup of tea?"

Nicci half turned to look up at Agnes. Her look said she thought Agnes the doddering old woman she had been pretending to be.

Agnes drove the sharp points of the knitting needles into the spot where Nicci's heart should have been.

Nicci reared back in surprise and Agnes was able to take the gun from her fingers. She'd never liked guns and would be glad when she could turn it over to the sheriff as soon as he arrived.

Blood bubbled from Nicci's lips. "I should have known it would be you," she said and reached for Agnes as if grasping for her throat to strangle her.

Agnes took a step back and waited, making sure that when Nicci went down this time, she wouldn't be getting back up.

Epilogue

"A triple wedding?" Kate cried and clapped her hands together laughing.

"Why not?" Dalton said, smiling over at his bride-to-be.

Georgia met his gaze, her brown eyes shining with happiness. "Why not? We all discussed it," she said, glancing around the Trails West Ranch table. Both Maddie and Faith nodded and echoed her words. "We think it will be wonderful."

"We're all going to be one big happy family so why not start with one big happy family wedding?" Dalton said, sounding as happy as he felt. He never dreamed after Nicci that he could ever have a happy ever after.

"A big happy family," quipped Lantry.

Grayson raised his margarita glass in a toast. "To my sons and their beautiful brides-to-be."

Everyone chimed in.

Dalton looked around the room at his family, his gaze coming back to Georgia. He had what he always wanted, a sense of belonging to something greater than himself, being accepted and most of all, being loved.

He couldn't believe it. He was still pinching himself. He never dreamed this possible. But he and Georgia had shed the weight of the past. They were both looking to a future, anxious to start their lives together.

Because of everything that had happened to them, they didn't want to spend another minute apart.

"I got a postcard today from Agnes," Georgia said retrieving it from her pocket. "I think you'd better read it to everyone." She handed the card to Dalton, who frowned and read out loud:

"Having a great time on my extended vacation in the islands, but plan to be back for the wedding at the end of the month. Regards to Maddie and Faith. I saw your triple wedding in a dream. It is going to be beautiful!

Your friend, Agnes."

Dalton looked up at Georgia. "Did you tell her—"

"Tonight was the first time Maddie and I and Faith even discussed a triple wedding, and as you can see Agnes's postcard was mailed over a week ago."

Dalton laughed, shaking his head. "There is no one like Agnes. Do you know she asked the sheriff for her knitting needles back after he closed the investigation. She said they were her lucky ones."

Everyone laughed.

"She is one amazing woman," Georgia said. "She saved our lives."

"And then she decided to live a little by going on this tropical island vacation," Dalton added.

"You know, I was thinking I'd like to ask her to be one of my bridesmaids," Georgia said, reaching for Dalton's hand. "If it's all right with you."

He beamed at her. "Of course."

"I'll have to get word to her," Georgia said, then laughed. "But I have a feeling she might already know."

THE WHITEHORSE SEWING CIRCLE would be talking for years about the triple wedding of Dalton Corbett and Georgia Michaels, Shane Corbett and Maddie Cavanaugh, and Jud Corbett and Faith Bailey.

"It was the most beautiful thing I have ever seen," said Pearl Cavanaugh, whose mother had founded the sewing circle years before.

"I don't know about the rest of you, but I cried when I saw those three brides come out," confessed Alice Miller, one of the oldest of the group. "They couldn't have been more beautiful."

"And Agnes, you were a sight for sore eyes," Lila Bailey Jackson said. She had come back for her daughter Faith's wedding and decided to stay a few days after saying she'd missed the quilting group.

"I loved your dress. It was so…different from most bridesmaids dresses but then you weren't the usual bridesmaid, now were you?" Ella said.

Agnes smiled. "It was the dress I wore when I married my Norbert, God rest his soul. It was Georgia's idea that I wear something that meant the most to me."

"Well it was certainly an exciting wedding," Pearl said as she took a stitch and smiled in memory. "The matron of honor having her baby right after the ceremony put quite the exclamation point on things."

"Have you seen Rory's baby? Devlin Jr. is adorable. Ten pounds, four ounces," Alice said. "We finished his baby quilt just in time."

Everyone chuckled since the Whitehorse Sewing

Circle had been making a quilt for each new baby, since it had begun.

"Whose baby quilt are we starting on next?" Arlene Evans asked.

The women glanced at one another around the table.

"After that wedding, I think we'd better plan on making three in the next nine months," Pearl said. "Those Corbett brides all had that certain look in their eyes. Amazing, but I think the population of Whitehorse is about to grow and I wouldn't be surprised if there was another wedding before long," she said, looking over at Arlene, who only smiled shyly and took another stitch.

* * * * *

INTRIGUE..

INTRIGUE...

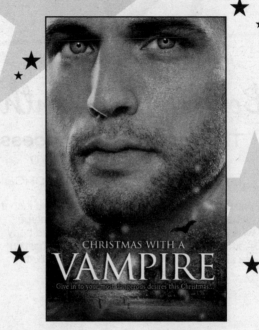

Meet Nora Robert's
The MacGregors family

1st October 2010

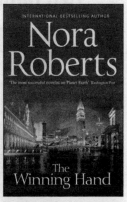

3rd December 2010

7th January 2011

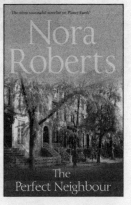

4th February 2011

"Did you say I won almost two million dollars?"

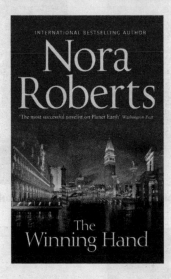

Down to her last ten dollars in a Las Vegas casino, Darcy Wallace gambled and won!

Suddenly the small-town girl was big news— and needing protection. Robert MacGregor Blade, the casino owner, was determined to make sure Darcy could enjoy her good fortune. But Darcy knew what she wanted; Mac himself. Surely her luck was in?

Available 3rd December 2010

www.millsandboon.co.uk

A Christmas bride for the cowboy

Two classic love stories by bestselling author
Diana Palmer in one Christmas collection!

Featuring

Sutton's Way
and
Coltrain's Proposal

Available 3rd December 2010

All the magic you'll need this Christmas...

When **Daniel** is left with his brother's kids, only one person can help. But it'll take more than mistletoe before **Stella** helps him...

Patrick hadn't advertised for a housekeeper. But when **Hayley** appears, she's the gift he didn't even realise he needed.

Alfie and his little sister know a lot about the magic of Christmas – and they're about to teach the grown-ups a much-needed lesson!

Available 1st October 2010

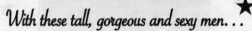

2 FREE BOOKS
AND A SURPRISE GIFT

We would like to take this opportunity to thank you for reading this Mills & Boon® book by offering you the chance to take TWO more specially selected books from the Intrigue series absolutely FREE! We're also making this offer to introduce you to the benefits of the Mills & Boon® Book Club™—

- **FREE home delivery**
- **FREE gifts and competitions**
- **FREE monthly Newsletter**
- **Exclusive Mills & Boon Book Club offers**
- **Books available before they're in the shops**

Accepting these FREE books and gift places you under no obligation to buy, you may cancel at any time, even after receiving your free books. Simply complete your details below and return the entire page to the address below. You don't even need a stamp!

YES Please send me 2 free Intrigue books and a surprise gift. I understand that unless you hear from me, I will receive 5 superb new stories every month, including two 2-in-1 books priced at £5.30 each and a single book priced at £3.30, postage and packing free. I am under no obligation to purchase any books and may cancel my subscription at any time. The free books and gift will be mine to keep in any case.

Ms/Mrs/Miss/Mr _____ Initials _____

Surname _____

Address _____

_____

_____ Postcode _____

E-mail _____

Send this whole page to: Mills & Boon Book Club, Free Book Offer, FREEPOST NAT 10298, Richmond, TW9 1BR